— PROLOGUE —

The Unicorn Incident

The Unicorns arrived right after the buses.

I could just see them from my classroom window if I leaned really far over my desk and craned my neck. The trailers they came in had the words *EverSun Unicorn Farms* printed on the side. If I leaned farther—

"Pip!" my father said as my elbow accidentally knocked a box of rocks onto the ground.

"Whoops," I replied in a sorry sort of way and ducked to collect them.

My father didn't normally come to school with me. But today was Career Day. The halls and classrooms were full of mothers and fathers eager to talk about their jobs. Both of my parents were geologists, which was why Dad had brought the box of rocks (he called them *geodes*) to show my classmates. Studying rocks wasn't really my thing, but I felt like my dad was still a lot cooler than the parent who made zippers.

But let's face it—*nothing* was as cool as the Unicorns.

Through the window, I saw a woman in a bright blue shirt unload the first Unicorn. It felt a little like my heart and brain were exploding into Unicorn-shaped fireworks. Thanks to my favorite book, *Jeffrey Higgleston's Guide to Magical Creatures* (which I happened to have in my backpack right at that moment), I knew all about Unicorns.

I didn't get to see Unicorns all that often—they were pretty rare in the middle of Atlanta. This particular Unicorn was all shimmery, with a sunshine-colored mane and dark, rolling eyes. As it pranced over the asphalt, sparks flew up from beneath its butter-colored hooves.

"Oh, Unicorns!" my father said in the same voice I used whenever he showed me some new sort of rock—which is to say, he was trying his hardest to sound interested, but in the end, animals just weren't his thing. "How exciting. Who do they belong to?"

I pointed to Marisol Barrera, who sat four seats away from me. My father made an approving noise. Everyone approved of Marisol. She never had chocolate on her cheek. She remembered to brush her hair. Her handwriting was neat. The corners of her homework folders were never crumpled. She wore a blue shirt that matched her mother's, with a tiny, colorful EverSun logo.

Pip Bartlett's

• GUIDE TO •

MAGICAL CREATURES

— A NOVEL BY —

JACKSON PEARCE *AND* MAGGIE STIEFVATER

SCHOLASTIC

Scholastic Children's Books
An imprint of Scholastic Ltd
Euston House, 24 Eversholt Street, London, NW1 1DB, UK
Registered office: Westfield Road, Southam, Warwickshire, CV47 0RA
SCHOLASTIC and associated logos are trademarks and/or
registered trademarks of Scholastic Inc.

First published in the US by Scholastic Inc, 2015
First published in the UK by Scholastic Ltd, 2015

Text copyright © Jackson Pearce and Maggie Stiefvater, 2015
Illustrations copyright © Maggie Stiefvater, 2015

The right of Jackson Pearce and Maggie Stiefvater to be identified as the
authors and illustrator of this work has been asserted by them.

ISBN 978 1407 14862 5

Printed by CPI Group (UK) Ltd, Croydon, CR0 4YY
Papers used by Scholastic Children's Books are made
from wood grown in sustainable forests.

1 3 5 7 9 10 8 6 4 2

This is a work of fiction. Names, characters, places, incidents
and dialogues are products of the author's imagination or are used
fictitiously. Any resemblance to actual people, living or dead,
events or locales is entirely coincidental.

www.scholastic.co.uk

Book design by Christopher Stengel

Unicorn

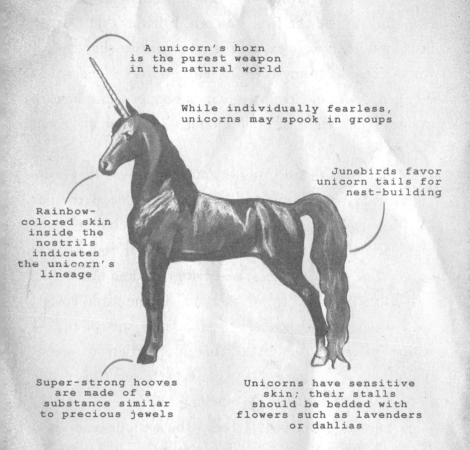

A unicorn's horn is the purest weapon in the natural world

While individually fearless, unicorns may spook in groups

Junebirds favor unicorn tails for nest-building

Rainbow-colored skin inside the nostrils indicates the unicorn's lineage

Super-strong hooves are made of a substance similar to precious jewels

Unicorns have sensitive skin; their stalls should be bedded with flowers such as lavenders or dahlias

SIZE: 30–80"
WEIGHT: 400–3,200 lbs.
DESCRIPTION: Of all of the magical animals, the Unicorn is the most famous, and rightly so. This noble and bold creature comes in all shapes and colors, boasts populations on every continent, and has been the stuff of legend for centuries. These vibrant companions are prized for their looks and

I tried to sit up straighter, like Marisol, but my back-bone couldn't sort out how to do it. I ended up slouching.

Oh, well. At least there was one thing I could do that Marisol couldn't. I didn't think *anyone* else could do it, actually. I could talk to magical creatures. *And they could understand me.*

No one believed me about this, unfortunately. Also, I didn't get a lot of practice with it, since the building where I lived didn't allow animals of any kind—even magical ones.

I hadn't ever gotten to talk to a Unicorn before.

"All right, everyone!" Mr. Dyatlov, our teacher, called. "We're going to line up in an *orderly fashion* to see some of the careers outdoors. Let's show our parents how good we can be!"

Mr. Dyatlov was all about orderly. Everything about him was a straight line—his haircut, his mustache, his tie, even his mouth. We learned pretty early in the school year that life was easier if you were as orderly as possible, so we lined up as straight as his eyebrows. In only minutes I'd be face-to-face with the Unicorns. I tried not to dance too much in line, but even after I convinced my heart to stop thumping, my feet kept tapping.

I couldn't be calm!

Especially not once we got to the parking lot, which was full of unusual things. An antiques dealer had brought a very old, strange-looking car. A florist stood beside a van with a pop-up tent full of flowers. A chef dad had set up a grill. A group of moms played stringed instruments. My father set up his box of geodes, which a bunch of my friends were already peeking into. Dad looked pleased, like he'd hatched the rocks instead of finding them.

I counted the Unicorns. There were eight of them! Marisol's mom and dad and their twin grown-up daughters each held the leads of two Unicorns. They looked regal and beautiful. The Barreras, I mean—they were the adult versions of Marisol, all polished and well dressed and wearing clothes that looked like they'd just had the tags popped off.

The Unicorns? Well. They looked *magical*.

"Students! Students!" Mr. Dyatlov said. "Remember— we each need to rotate to every station. And what's the Outdoor Time rule?"

"No running, no going off on our own, and wash our hands when we get back inside!" we all repeated obediently. Satisfied, Mr. Dyatlov waved us off, and we all walked—very, very, very fast—to our first stations.

Obviously, I was going to the Unicorns first. It worked

out pretty well too, since the chef parent was luring everyone in his direction with hot-off-the-griddle pancakes. I would have some time at the Unicorn station by myself!

"Hi there!" Marisol's mom said, smiling at me as I approached. "Do you think you want to raise Unicorns when you grow up?"

"Yes! I mean, maybe! I mean, I don't know—I just love Unicorns! All animals, really," I said breathlessly, gazing at the eight Unicorns. They were each just a little different—a pink mane on this one, a green one on that one. Their hooves were different colors too, and while they all had light-colored bodies, some were a bluish shade and others were more peachy. They each had a perfectly spiraled, pearly horn sprouting from the center of their foreheads.

"It's the strongest substance on earth, you know," one of Marisol's sisters said when she saw me staring at the nearest Unicorn's horn.

"I know! Can I touch it?" I asked.

"Sure!" Ms. Barrera said, but she didn't understand—I wasn't asking *her* permission. I was asking the Unicorn's.

"Always nice to meet a fan," the Unicorn said in a deep male voice. Then he snorted a bit and lowered his head. Since the Barreras couldn't hear what the Unicorn said to me—I was the only one who could—they looked a little surprised that he was letting me touch him. But I had asked nicely, after all. I reached out and touched the edge of the horn. It felt like the inside of a seashell.

The Unicorn snorted and lifted back up. His liquid eyes of dark magic had turned into liquid eyes of faint disapproval as he observed my untied shoes and wild hair. I guess he was used to people like the Barreras.

He said, "All right, that's enough. They just polished it. I don't want you to get it *grimy*."

"Oh. Sorry," I said.

"For what, dear?" Ms. Barrera said.

"I think I bothered your Unicorn," I told her.

Ms. Barrera chuckled. "Don't mind Fortnight. He's the oldest member of our herd—he can be a little moody. Melody, bring Raindancer over here! She's a little more kid-friendly."

Raindancer whinnied happily as she was led forward. "Oh, yay! Look! Now everyone will see my tail!" The other Unicorns muttered and rolled their eyes as she made a show of swishing her tail back and forth. But it *was* a very impressive tail—all ringlet-shaped, turquoise curls.

"It's very pretty!" I said.

"*Thank you!*" Raindancer replied. "They spent all morning curling it to test the style before our next show. I think it suits me, don't you?"

"Definitely," I said. "Can they do your mane like that too?"

"That would take *hours*," Raindancer told me. "I can't stand still that long!"

I knew exactly how she felt. "Me neither."

The Barreras eyed me. Of course, they couldn't hear Raindancer's side of the conversation, so I seemed to be talking to myself.

"She was telling me about her tail," I explained.

"Of course she was," Ms. Barrera said politely. But she was wearing the eyebrows-raised, half smile that meant, *This child is crazy*. I wished I could get used to that face, but I never did. Magical creatures were a lot more accepting of my power than other humans were. Why couldn't people just believe me?

"Rotate stations!" Mr. Dyatlov called out, and everyone began to shuffle around. A big group of Marisol and about six other kids hurried over from the pancake station. I should have moved on to the dad who had brought a blowtorch and welding mask, but I pretended like I hadn't heard Mr. Dyatlov and stayed with the Unicorns.

"They're amazing, Marisol!" someone called out.

"Thanks!" Marisol said.

The appearance of so many kids definitely affected the Unicorns. They began tossing their heads and blowing out their nostrils, revealing rainbow-colored skin inside. One of them said, "Look at me!" and another said, "No, look at *me*!" Even Fortnight half reared and said in a low voice, "No, they are all looking at *me*."

I hadn't ever realized that show Unicorns were really *show-off* Unicorns.

Raindancer was thrashing her ringlet-filled tail and craning her neck to check if anyone had noticed it yet. She shoved her muzzle against my arm. "You there—you! The one who can talk to us. Ask those children what they think of my tail!"

I wasn't really great at talking in front of lots of people, but this was basically my first Unicorn encounter, and I didn't want to disappoint her. Raising my voice, I asked, "Hey, everyone! What do you think of that Unicorn's tail?"

But everyone was pelting the Barreras with questions. No one heard me. Raindancer flipped her mane in irritation. As the children got louder, the Unicorns did too. "Child! Child! Look at me! Look over here! No, here! Child!"

Marisol tugged on her mother's hand. "Mom, can my friends go for a ride on Fortnight?"

Ms. Barrera shook her head. "I don't think that's a good idea. Maybe *you* could take him around the court-yard, just to show everyone."

"Not *him*!" shouted four of the Unicorns in unison. "Pick *me*!"

Mr. Barrera switched Fortnight's simple halter for a special silver bridle with a cutout for the horn. As Ms. Barrera gave Marisol a leg up, Fortnight chewed thoughtfully on the bit, which looked as if it was made out of crystal. He didn't seem at all concerned that Marisol might be grimy. Seated on the back of the biggest, most beautiful Unicorn of them all, Marisol looked like an honest-to-goodness princess.

Everyone was looking at her.

"Can she make him run?" one of my classmates shouted.

"*Run?* Not exactly. Unicorns have five gaits, unlike horses, which only have four," Ms. Barrera said. "They are called *walk*, *prance*, *mince*, *frolic*, and *gallop*. I think it's only safe for walking and prancing in a crowd like this."

Marisol and Fortnight began to prance. It was so beautiful I had to close and unclose my hands into fists a bunch of times to distract myself. I had thought everyone was looking at her before. But now all eyes were *really* on her.

Raindancer punched my arm with her muzzle again. "Hey! You! Child-talker!"

"That hurts," I told her, even though it didn't.

"Look at how they're all watching him," Raindancer complained. "That should be me! Tell them it should be me!"

"No one listens to me," I said. Fortnight had gotten a little excited with all of the attention and had begun to mince, but Marisol expertly reined him back in.

"Me either!" Raindancer's hooves clattered. Sparks flew up. "Child-talker! Climb onto my back! We'll show them!"

Climb onto my back!

I knew it was a terrible idea. But—but—*riding a Unicorn*. I'd only read about it in the *Guide*. When would I ever get another chance to actually *do* it?

My mother was always telling me, *Think twice, act once.*

And I *was* thinking. I really was. But it was hard to think about anything other than riding a Unicorn, especially while Raindancer was saying, louder and louder, "Do-it-do-it-do-it-do-it-do-it—"

I thought twice and acted once. Raindancer ducked down and I scrambled onto her back.

She shouted, "Hold on to my mane, grimy Child-talker!"

I just had time to grab two big fistfuls of her swimming-pool-colored mane before she reared and sang out a whinny.

Now all eyes were on *us*.

"What are you doing?" snapped Fortnight, nearly unseating Marisol. "This is my moment! Get back to the others, you silly filly!"

"SILLY FILLY?" roared Raindancer. "Watch this!"

She plunged forward. I wasn't sure what gait she had selected, but it felt a lot speedier than a prance or a mince. It was definitely either a frolic or a gallop. I could see the fancy old car and the pancake grills and the florist van getting farther away than I wanted—

"We have to stay in the courtyard!" I urged her, clinging on tightly to her mane.

"Oh, right-right-right," she sang out. Slowing, she wheeled back toward the crowd, frolicking in an enormous, beautiful circle. Her ringlet tail snapped behind her. The wind cascaded over my ears and whipped at my ponytail. It felt like I was flying. I could just glimpse the envious gazes of my classmates.

It was the best day ever.

"Pip!"

I thought I heard my name, but it was lost in the joyful rush of air. I imagined that I too looked like a princess, as Raindancer whirled her ringlets once more.

"I am the most beautiful-beautiful-beautiful!" she called, in time with her hoofbeats.

I slowly realized people were calling my name. Many people.

"Pip!" shouted Ms. Barrera. "Try to come back! Unicorns don't do well in groups; the others are going to spook if we don't calm Raindancer down!"

I knew that—it was in the *Guide*, about Unicorns spooking in groups. But *spooking* meant *panicking*, and these Unicorns weren't panicking. They were shouting, "No fair! Why does she get to go out? I'm going out there! Let me go!"

They weren't scared. They were jealous.

I should really make a note of that in the Guide, I thought, just as one of the other Unicorns broke free from a Barrera twin.

"You're blocking the view!" Raindancer screamed at the newcomer. It was not a very attractive scream. "Of *me*!"

"Don't be such a *donkey*," neighed the new Unicorn, jostling into Raindancer's haunches. He was a handsome blond Unicorn with smooth skin like a dolphin. He flipped his white corn-silk mane, and a few butterflies fell out. They looked a little surprised. "You have to share!"

"You aren't the boss of me!" Raindancer snorted.

"Guys!" I called. "Guys, don't fight, you're both beautiful! Boy Unicorn, you need to go back!"

"*You* aren't the boss of *me*!" He bucked and jostled into Raindancer again. I clutched her mane more tightly.

"Pip! Hold on!" shouted Ms. Barrera. "Be calm, honey! We'll get you down from there!"

They thought I was in trouble.

"OOF!" Raindancer shouted as another Unicorn bashed into her on the other side. A third Unicorn with a mane the color of green Popsicles twirled his horn around a big hank of Raindancer's tail ringlets. He tossed his head and nearly jerked her off her feet. The Barreras were all waving their arms as if they were drowning in a concrete sea. None of them was holding a Unicorn, because all of the Unicorns were rearing and stampeding around Raindancer.

Maybe I *was* in trouble.

"Raindancer, we need to go back," I said. "Everyone's seen your tail! But we can't—"

"OH, YES, THE CHILDREN ARE LOOKING AT ME NOW!" shouted Fortnight, drowning out my voice. He pranced and flicked his tail wildly, nearly throwing Marisol off his back, then cried, "BEHOLD, YOU HORNED BRATS! THEY MARVEL OVER ME!"

The other Unicorns and I beheld him. The children weren't so much marveling as goggling, because a herd of

Unicorns was now barreling straight toward them. Parents and teachers began to snatch students out of the way.

"Raindancer!" I tried again, raising my voice. "Don't you want them to be happy with you?"

"I want them to *look*!" Raindancer said. She snapped her teeth at the blond Unicorn. The Barreras and a few other adults had linked hands and were approaching on one side of the milling herd, like a human fence.

"Turn her in small circles!" Marisol shouted to me. She had pulled one of Fortnight's reins very short, so he was being forced to turn in smaller and smaller circles. It was slowing him down.

"I don't have any reins!" I howled back.

The other Unicorns were now laughing themselves breathless over Fortnight's little circles as they increased their speed.

"So long, old man!" shouted Raindancer. "Watch this, everyone!"

And she leaped. I made an *eep* sound and threw my arms around her neck.

Sparks flew as Raindancer landed on top of the fancy antique car. Someone screamed. Another Unicorn hurtled up next to us, and a third Unicorn with pink hair sailed right on over the car and careened into the florist's tent instead. The pink-haired Unicorn thrashed her head around, covering herself with tattered bits of flowers. When the florist dad tried to shoo her off with a sunflower, she grabbed it in her mouth and danced away with it.

"Admire me! Admire! Admire!" she shouted as she waved it back and forth, swatting my classmates in the process.

Fortnight, who I guess had had enough of being teased, unseated Marisol and galloped toward Raindancer, leaping into the air and arcing his back gracefully on the way. It was impressive, until he crashed through the grill and sent burgers skidding across the pavement. The blond Unicorn dodged the burgers but wound up stamping on the pancake tables, and batter slung through the sky and splattered across the moms with stringed instruments. All the running around upset my dad's table, and his geodes smashed to the ground. The ones that didn't break rolled under the hooves of the green-maned Unicorn, who stumbled. To avoid falling forward, the Unicorn sat down—on Mr. Dyatlov.

"Get off him!" I yelled. The Unicorn pranced away, but only because he'd noticed all the attention the sunflower-wielding Unicorn was getting. Mr. Dyatlov looked okay, though he'd been squished into the fallen hamburgers, which were now stuck to his pants.

"Raindancer, *stop*," I pleaded.

"Isn't this what you wanted? For everyone to look at you?" Raindancer whinnied.

"No!" I shouted back. "I wanted them to *listen* to me!"

But even Raindancer wasn't listening to me now. As a Unicorn with a mane that was sherbet-orange charged beside us, Raindancer charged directly through our school sign. Wood slivers sprayed everywhere. I saw the bit of wood with our mascot on it—a smiling gopher—go flying past my face. Raindancer sang gleefully.

Her hooves touched the ground with a massive jolt. I snatched for a better grip, but somehow my hands and her slippery mane seemed nowhere near each other.

I made another *eep* sound—Raindancer didn't so much as flick an ear—and landed in a decorative bush beside the smiling gopher. Through the broken branches, I could see the blue sky overhead. It was blocked out briefly by the bellies of three Unicorns as they jumped over both the broken sign and the bush I was now lying in.

All of my breath and happiness had been knocked out of me.

Just a minute later, my father appeared, panting for his own breath. "Pip! Pip! Are you *alive*?"

"I'm okay," I said from inside the bush.

"In that case," he said, "you're in so much trouble."

Silently, I decided to add another note to the *Guide to Magical Creatures*:

Unicorns are bad listeners.

CHAPTER
— 1 —

Cloverton Clinic for Magical Creatures

Okay, so maybe I wrecked Career Day and ruined Fortnight's show season and destroyed three cellos, forty perfectly good turkey burgers, most of Dad's geodes, and Mr. Dyatlov's glasses. It's not something I'm proud of, and getting grounded for the rest of the school year wasn't much fun. After the Unicorn Incident (which was what my mom called it when she went all narrow-eyed and frown-y), my parents decided that I should spend the summer in Cloverton, a little town in south Georgia, where my aunt Emma was a veterinarian for magical creatures.

"This way you can see lots of magical creatures in a . . . erm . . . *safer* environment," Mom said as she packed my purple suitcase. I think by "safer" she meant "place with fewer cellos."

Since Mom had to go on a very important geological dig and Dad had just left to give a presentation, one of Mom's interns, Shantel, drove me to Cloverton. Aunt

Pip Bartlett

Ponytail hides the days when she forgets to brush her hair

Brain is stuffed full of magical animal facts, maps of places she's been, and flavors of sandwich cookies she's eaten

Best book ever

Best book EVER

BEST BOOK EVER

Jeffrey Higgleston's Guide to Magical Creatures

Sometimes has writing on her hands because if she has no paper, she has to write on SOMETHING

Mini-flashlight in this pocket

Pen in this pocket

Patch with the logo of the American Academy of Magical Beasts

Sandwich cookies in this pocket

Her father sewed the pockets all over these pants (he's really good at sewing) (he also put patches on her Scout vest) (until she got kicked out for an unfortunate incident involving Flying Dachshunds)

Heart patch from her mother

Marshmallows in this pocket (because they are good snacks for over 20 species of magical creatures) (also for girls)

SIZE: 52"
AGE: 9 years
DESCRIPTION: This particular human, "Pip Bartlett," seems to be the only person alive who can understand what magical animals are saying. Also she is not very happy with Unicorns at the moment.

Emma's house was attached to the clinic, but it didn't seem right to just stroll into her living room without saying hello to her first, so Shantel and I went to the clinic instead.

"Hmm, she must be with a patient," Shantel said—there was no one at the reception desk and no sign of Aunt Emma in the waiting room. "Do you want me to stay until she comes out?" Shantel asked. She didn't look like she wanted to.

"No, I can wait by myself," I said. How much trouble could I get into in a waiting room?

Shantel gave me a thumbs-up. "Great." Then she hurried outside and peeled out of the parking lot at the speed of a runaway Unicorn. In the waiting room, I shoved my backpack under a chair and sat on my hands to keep myself still. The only other person in the waiting room was a friendly looking young man with a shirt (plaid) and a beard (not plaid). He had a Lilac-Horned Pomeranian on a leash. I could tell it was elderly because the lilac fur around its nose was now bluish silver.

"Can I pet her?" I asked.

He nodded. "If she'll let you. Missy gets a little nervous at the vet."

The Lilac-Horned Pomeranian's tongue darted out to lick my hand as I patted the tuft of fur between her horns.

"It's okay, Missy. There's nothing to be nervous about. My aunt Emma is very nice." While her owner didn't realize it, Missy understood me perfectly, and looked a little happier as she retreated back under her owner's chair.

It was good to know that talking to animals didn't always end up with a stampede.

To be honest, though, I was a little nervous too. My aunt Emma was indeed very nice, but I really wasn't sure what she thought of me since the Unicorn Incident.

I picked up a brochure from the table beside me. It was called "Easy Nutrition for Newborn Pegasi." The front featured a picture of a winged horse flying over an empty dinner plate. Even before I opened it, I knew that the plate should have been piled with peanut butter. Peanut butter, especially the chunky kind, is a baby Pegasus's favorite food, according to *Jeffrey Higgleston's Guide to Magical Creatures*. Chapter three, page four.

My copy of the *Guide* was in my backpack, as always—I insisted on carrying it there, with my sandwich cookies and spare pens. I liked having it close by.

The old bell above the door dinged. I looked up as two women struggled in with a large plastic animal crate.

Oh.

Oh!

It was a HobGrackle! I'd never seen one in real life

Juvenile Pegasus

Multicolored in adulthood, particularly in warm climates. As newborn Pegasi can weigh up to 75 pounds, adults build nests in particularly strong trees, such as oaks and redwoods.

Juvenile Pegasi are voracious, with an affinity for nut butters, especially chunky peanut butter. They also enjoy mashed-up bananas. Oddly enough, field researchers have discovered that both adult and juvenile Pegasi will happily eat plastic wrap if given the opportunity. Studies show that Pegasi deprived of free before. Inside the crate, a shiny beak tapped anxiously on the metal cage bars. The beak was black, but black like a pool of oil—swirled with other colors too. Rainbow-y. But the beak wasn't how I could tell it was a HobGrackle. It was the—

"What is that *smell*?" said Callie from behind the check-in desk.

Callie was my thirteen-year-old cousin. We'd hung out together on family vacations, but weren't exactly friends, because Callie liked musicals with lots of costumes and dancing and I liked Lilac-Horned Pomeranians and biting my nails. Those things weren't opposites, but they kind of felt like it when you were trying to strike up a friendly conversation.

"Oh, sorry," said the lady at the front of the crate. "That's Goggy."

According to the *Guide to Magical Creatures*, HobGrackles release an odor "similar to that of a rotting ostrich egg on a sidewalk" when they are stressed.

This HobGrackle smelled pretty stressed.

The *Guide* said the smell came from a slippery, oily sweat that was released from the HobGrackle's armpits. And leg pits. And chin. And tail pit. I wasn't sure what a tail pit was, but any oily substance that came from it seemed like a bad idea.

"Goggy's been limping," one of the women said to Callie. "I don't know what's going on with him. Maybe you could just—"

Callie interrupted the woman by popping her gum and slapping the sign-up sheet with a pencil. "Sign in."

The woman looked a little stressed herself. "Goggy isn't great at waiting. Are there many patients ahead of us?"

Callie gave her a bored look through her bright pink glasses. "Let me break it down for you, lady. There's a feverish Miniature Silky Griffin in exam room one. I've got an Invisible Salamander vomiting up socks in exam room two. There's a litter of levitating Garden Trolls in room three that need their shots. *Goggy* doesn't have an appointment. *Goggy* will have to sign in. *Goggy* will have to wait."

"Okay," the woman said meekly.

I pretend-drew on my hand, avoiding Callie's eyes. It was nice to see that grown women found Callie as scary as I did.

The door dinged again, and I looked up excitedly—first a HobGrackle, now what?

But the lady who walked in didn't seem to have a magical creature with her. Instead, she had pointy shoes, angry eyebrows, and a clipboard tucked under her arm. She marched up to Callie, and when she passed I got a whiff of some sort of perfume that smelled like a field of wilting gardenias. It was a lot worse than the way Goggy smelled, if you ask me. I tried to cover my nose without being too impolite. The Lilac-Horned Pomeranian whistled sadly.

The lady smacked her clipboard on the counter in front of Callie. "I'm here to do an inspection on . . . some sort of Invisible Salamander thing?"

"Hello, Mrs. Dreadbatch," Callie said, her voice suddenly very calm and very proper and very unlike the voice she'd just used with Goggy's owners. "I'll get my mom for you in just a moment. She's busy right now with—"

"Busy!" Dreadbatch snorted and put a hand on her hip. "She'd better not be too busy for an official visit from the Supernatural/Magical Animal Care, Keeping, and Education Department!"

My heart stopped. Well, paused. I knew all about the Supernatural/Magical Animal Care, Keeping, and Education Department—S.M.A.C.K.E.D. They were the government department in charge of making sure that magical creatures didn't get in the way of regular, non-magical life. They had visited our school the day after the Unicorn Incident, and they'd nearly had Raindancer taken away from the Barreras. They *would* have taken her away, actually, if I hadn't said that it was all my fault.

Remembering that horrible afternoon made my heart stay paused for a little longer.

Callie's voice rose. "You have to understand that—"

"I'm a very busy woman, young lady," Dreadbatch interrupted, waving her off, "and if I can't complete the S.M.A.C.K.E.D. paperwork showing that steps are being taken to prevent the Invisible Salamander from eating the laundry off everyone's lines again, it'll have to be labeled a public nuisance. And you know what *that* means."

"Yes, his owner will have to get rid of him," Callie snapped, sounding more like her normal self. "I know. I know. I *know*. Hold on, I'll see if Mom can get away from the Griffin."

After Callie had gone into the back, the waiting room went very quiet, except for the rap-rap-rap of Dreadbatch's long, coral-colored nails drumming on the reception desk. Either the noise or her perfume didn't seem to be having a good effect on the animals in the waiting room. Both the Lilac-Horned Pomeranian and the HobGrackle were looking at Dreadbatch and quivering. Something thin and purple oozed onto the tile floor from the bottom of the HobGrackle's crate: HobGrackle sweat. It coated the metal bars and smelled even more like rotten eggs than before.

I frowned.

The *Guide* observed that HobGrackles really made terrible pets—what with the oozing and the claws and the beak and the diet of rats and all that—but that didn't stop people from trying. Jeffrey Higgleston insisted they had great personalities. But he'd said something else about them, something I couldn't quite remember . . .

The oily door of the crate burst into the air. Goggy shot out. The clinic was suddenly full of miscellaneous screams.

Then I remembered: The sweat of a stressed HobGrackle could *melt metal*.

Goggy scampered across three empty chairs, knocking them all over. He looked just like the illustration in the *Guide*: He had a bird's beak, but a pit bull's head. His furry wings were brindle, as were his legs, which were an equal mixture of fur and tiny feathers. His tail was much, much longer than the rest of him—yards and yards of rope-like tail that uncoiled from the crate, finally ending in a tuft of fur and feathers. It whipped his owners in the face, then knocked over three more office chairs.

My frown deepened.

Jeffrey Higgleston hadn't mentioned the tail.

Goggy leaped for the closed glass door of the clinic. He smacked into it with the sort of crash you'd expect when a winged animal runs straight into a glass door. He left a big smear of egg-smelling HobGrackle spit on the glass. Then he climbed up the wall, tearing paintings off their hooks.

Dreadbatch looked horrified. *"Control your monster!"* she screeched, holding up her clipboard like a shield.

"Goggy!" wailed his owner. "HEEL!"

Goggy did not heel. He ran around the walls with no apparent regard for gravity, leaving purple footprints.

"Goggy!" I shouted. "You have to stop!"

"No, I have to *flee*!" Goggy cried. "Flee! The mean lady will take you away from your owners! She'll lock you up! She'll send you away! *Flee!*"

"I'm reporting this to S.M.A.C.K.E.D.!" Dreadbatch yelled, which made Goggy's owners panic, which made Goggy panic even *more*. Plus, now the Lilac-Horned Pomeranian was freaking out—

"Missy!" I pleaded. "Not you too! Everyone just calm down!"

"What's happening here?" Callie exclaimed as she reappeared behind the desk. She looked at Goggy, then Dreadbatch, then, finally, me. I was worried that she would blame me, but she looked like she hated us all equally in that moment.

"A very illuminating event!" Dreadbatch said, her voice loud enough to be heard over the howls of animals and the weeping of Goggy's owners. "That's what is happening!"

Her voice sent Goggy into a fresh wave of panic. He clawed at the window and yelled, "We've got to get out of here!"

"Save yourself!" Missy cried, using her center horn to ram the door of the clinic. The bearded man tried to haul her back in by her leash, but she hunkered her weight down and rammed it again. Shards of glass went flying.

"A menace," Dreadbatch continued. "A danger to society—"

Goggy bounded off the window. One of his owners grabbed for his foot but missed; it was enough to knock him off-balance mid-leap. He twisted in the air, tail spiraling, purple sweat raining down—

And landed right in Dreadbatch's arms.

Everyone froze. Goggy dripped.

Dreadbatch screamed.

"We're all right, everyone!" a new voice called. It was calm, cheery, and totally *wrong* because (a) nothing about this was all right, (b) Goggy's sweat was now eating its way through the watch on Dreadbatch's wrist, and (c) Missy had a pretty sizable piece of the front door stuck on her center horn.

"We're all right!" the voice repeated.

It was Aunt Emma. Since I had last seen her, she had cut her brown hair very short and dyed a single, choppy lock of it bright pink. She wore pink scrubs that were not quite as pink as her hair. Sweeping through the room, she gathered Goggy with one hand and offered Dreadbatch a towel with the other. Dreadbatch's eyebrows descended low over her eyes, but she accepted the towel.

Aunt Emma slipped Missy's leash out of the bearded man's hand, then said, "Callie, please get Mrs. Dreadbatch some hand sanitizer and order her a new watch. Ms. Webster, see if you can use the zip ties in the top right drawer of the work desk to put the door back on Goggy's crate for now. Mr. Rose, you look nervous, so why don't you go have a walk around the parking lot? Mrs. Dreadbatch, let me get these two critters sorted and I'll be back so we can go over that important paperwork. Everyone else, be patient, please!"

Aunt Emma was pretty good at fixing things, even though she couldn't talk with animals. Because her arms were full, she nudged at the door to the back room with her foot.

I jumped up to get the door for her. She blinked at me, like she was just now realizing I was there.

"Hi, Aunt Emma," I said meekly.

Aunt Emma smiled, and even though she looked a little harassed, it was a nice smile. "Hey there, Pip. Welcome to Cloverton."

CHAPTER
2

Purple Stuff in Armpits

"They really think I'm limping?" Goggy the HobGrackle asked. "That's why they brought me here?"

Goggy and I sat in exam room three (formerly occupied by the Troll babies), waiting for Aunt Emma, who was still chipping the glass off Missy's horn. Goggy was considerably calmer, in part because Dreadbatch wasn't in here, but mostly because he was exhausted from the chase around the clinic.

"That's what it says here on your chart," I said, nodding toward the clipboard. "You aren't limping?"

Goggy looked miffed. "I am learning ballet."

"You aren't hurt at all?"

"I'm hurt they didn't appreciate my interpretation of *Swan Lake*," Goggy sighed. He put his head down on his coiled-up tail. I took the opportunity to study him and finish the addition I'd made to the HobGrackle entry in *Jeffrey Higgleston's Guide to Magical Creatures*.

Common HobGrackle

Wings are capable, though the HobGrackle prefers perambulating to flight

HobGrackles have a blind spot below their beak—always approach animal from above or side to avoid startling it

Powerful beak for eating seeds and crushing lizards

Juvenile HobGrackles cannot fly until 8-9 months of age

very long tail = 15ft

HobGrackle fur is short, smooth, and brindled. If no brindle is present, check the ears. You may be looking at a Miniature Griffin, or a juvenile Rarefoot. If the latter: note venomous spines beneath tail.

Legs are protected by wiry guard hairs and warmed by downy feathers

---

SIZE: 29—34" at shoulder
WEIGHT: Males 30 lbs, females 60 lbs.
DESCRIPTION: The Common HobGrackle is one of four species of Hobs found in North America. The HobGrackle is best known for its purple perspiration, which it produces in copious quantities when under stress. Enthusiasts of the

It wasn't the first sketch or note that I'd added to the *Guide*. The foreword of the *Guide* said, "a good researcher will continue to study and discover magical creatures across the globe."

I very much wanted to be a good researcher.

The exam room door swung open and Aunt Emma walked in.

"Pip, your hair's gotten longer! I'm sorry about all that nonsense in the waiting room. Mrs. Dreadbatch . . . well . . . she doesn't have a very good *energy* with animals."

I thought that was a very nice way for Aunt Emma to put it.

Aunt Emma caught sight of my *Guide*. "I like your addition. I guess the HobGrackle chapter doesn't mention that tail, does it?"

She rubbed her head as she said this. Her hand had purple Goggy sweat on it and now her head did too, but she didn't appear too upset.

"I've never seen a HobGrackle before," I said quickly. "No one keeps them as pets in Atlanta, since they need so much space. I can't wait to see other magical creatures face-to-face."

"Oh, yes, your mom told me that you still really love them," Aunt Emma said. In a wistful voice, she added, "I wish Callie would take more of an interest—too bad there isn't a musical about magical animals, huh? Oh, well. I'm sure you'll learn a lot here."

"I really want to be helpful," I said. "Like Goggy, for instance. He's not actually limping! He was doing ballet! He told me."

Aunt Emma didn't respond right away. She didn't give me the look that meant, *This child is crazy*. But she did tilt her head a bit. Probably she was thinking about the Unicorn Incident.

Finally, she put a hand on my shoulder, leaving a small purple mark of HobGrackle sweat. "Pip. Kiddo. I know you love animals—especially magical ones. So do I! And I know sometimes it really does feel like they're talking to us. But do try to remember that it's only in your imagination. Animals need people like us precisely *because* they can't talk!"

"But, Aunt Emma, they talk—"

The exam room door opened and Callie walked in, looking about as friendly as a bag of Parisian Sparkle Vipers. She held a bucket of water and some purple-stained rags.

"Having a nice chat, I see? I could use some help," Callie said. "I'm not a miracle worker. I'm only one girl. One very overworked girl, forced to slave away every day

in her mother's place of business, barely getting an allowance, never getting a break to even spend the allowance,
basically giving up her childhood so that her mother can—"

"Okay, okay, Callie, that's a bit theatrical, don't you
think? What do you need?" Aunt Emma interrupted.

"Bubbles," Callie said. "He needs to be walked."

"I'll do it!" I piped up. I didn't know what Bubbles
was, but I was willing to take any excuse to make sure the
conversation about talking animals was done. I wanted to
be believed, but I wanted Aunt Emma to like me more.

Both Aunt Emma and Callie frowned at me. Well,
Callie was already frowning; she just frowned even more.

Aunt Emma said, "Maybe . . . I suppose I could call
Angelina and ask her son to join you. He's your age—we
thought you two might make good friends."

Callie snorted. "Good luck with that."

"Oh, I can go by myself," I said quickly. It wasn't that
I didn't *want* to have friends. I was just so much better at
talking to animals than people. I didn't know what Bubbles
was, but I knew it would be easier to talk with him than a
human stranger.

"I think you'll have more fun if you go with Tomas,"
Aunt Emma said firmly. "Besides, I don't like the idea
of you walking around the block by yourself. I don't want
you to get . . . misplaced."

"Lost," translated Callie. "Forever."

I had just come from Atlanta, which was a lot bigger than Cloverton, so I really didn't think I would get lost just walking around a block. But since I wasn't very good at talking to people, I *definitely* wasn't very good at arguing with them. So instead of trying to change Aunt Emma's mind, I asked, "What's Bubbles?"

Callie snorted again. "Come on."

Bubbles turned out to be a Griffin. To be more specific, he was a Miniature Silky Griffin.

To be *more* specific, he was a very *old* Miniature Silky Griffin who didn't like people, animals, or loud, soft, and medium noises. Callie pointed him out on top of a bookshelf in the record-keeping room. From the look of the shredded files around him, he'd been making a nest there.

"Don't drag him," Callie said, handing me a leash. "And don't let people get close to him. He's not friendly. Also, don't sing around him. He hates singing. Mom said Tomas will meet you at his mailbox. It's the one with the marigolds."

She whirled away.

"Bubbles?" I called up to him. "I'm Pip. Aunt Emma's niece. I'm supposed to take you for a walk."

"Finally," Bubbles said. His voice was crackly and old. He didn't sound surprised that I was talking directly to

Miniature Silky Griffin

Many owners choose to disbud their Griffins to protect other pets from accidental goring

Small wings mean that most are unable to fly, due to their love of table scraps and tendency to overeat

Velvet beak unique to smaller Griffin varieties

Soft, flowing hair must be carefully maintained to avoid matting

The hooves of the Miniature Silky Griffin must be trimmed once every six weeks to keep the Griffin from developing leg strain

Hooves smell like erasers

SIZE: 15" at shoulder
WEIGHT: Males 20 lbs, females 18 lbs.
DESCRIPTION: The Miniature Silky Griffin is the most popular variety of domestic Griffin. It was popularized by an Atlantic City gypsy dancer who kept several as pets and used them in her stage shows. Devoted, companionable, and trainable, they make excellent pets.

him. Hopping off the shelf, he glided down to the floor. The fur on his head was silvery around the edges, and the feathers that covered his back and wings were all sorts of colors, like a pile of leaves in the fall. I wanted to touch him to see if he was as silky as he looked, but I guessed from the cranky set of his ears that he wouldn't be very happy if I did.

So I just clipped the leash on to his harness and headed outside with him. I hadn't ever really thought about the smell of places, but Cloverton smelled very different from Atlanta. The scent of honeysuckle and hay wafted from the direction of the small stable where the large magical creatures were housed. I could also smell cookies baking from one of the nearby houses. It was nice. My parents weren't really the cookie-baking type—and it was pretty obvious Aunt Emma wasn't, or, if she was, she was too busy to actually bake cookies—but I liked the idea of other people baking cookies nearby.

As we walked down the clinic's long, flower-lined drive, I tried to make pleasant small talk with the Griffin. "Did you hear all the commotion with the HobGrackle?"

"HobGrackles," Bubbles sniffed. *"Purple."*

"Oh, he couldn't help it. Do you really hate singing?"

The Griffin gave me a beady-eyed glare. "Mostly just Callie's."

He grumbled to himself as we passed the buildings next to Cloverton Clinic for Magical Creatures. The clinic used to be a house, so it was mostly surrounded by other houses, some of which were now also businesses. Grown-up sorts of things, like lawyers or accountants or antique stores.

Standing in the street outside one of the houses that was still a house was a boy. Judging from the marigolds by his mailbox, this boy was Tomas.

Tomas was wiry and slight, with hands and glasses that looked two sizes too big for his body. He was so clean he was really quite shiny, though his hair stuck up like he'd rubbed it against a balloon. Tomas looked at me, then down at Bubbles, then back at me. I thought about how I'd describe him in the *Guide*.

I wasn't quite sure why my aunt and Tomas's mom thought we'd make good friends. He was about my age, sure, but judging from the look he was giving Bubbles, he wasn't a huge fan of animals. What would we talk about? I tried to think about Marisol and the sorts of things she would say to this boy.

"Why are you nervous?" Bubbles asked. I'd always heard Miniature Silky Griffins were particularly good at reading emotions, but I was still pretty impressed by how Bubbles hadn't even had to glance at me to pick up on it.

Tomas Ramirez

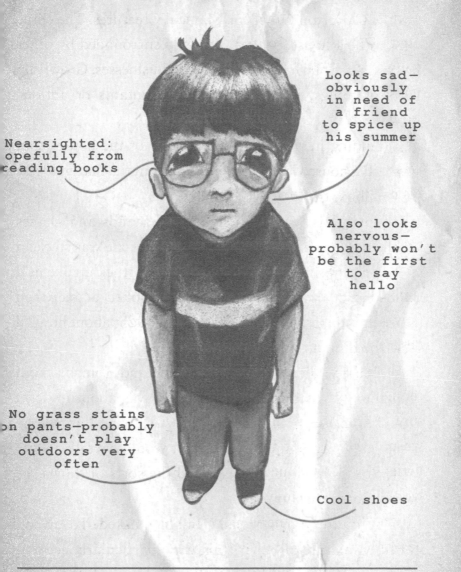

Looks sad—
obviously
in need of
a friend
to spice up
his summer

Nearsighted:
hopefully from
reading books

Also looks
nervous—
probably won't
be the first
to say
hello

No grass stains
on pants—probably
doesn't play
outdoors very
often

Cool shoes

SIZE: Smaller than me. But not by much.
WEIGHT: Won't blow away.
DESCRIPTION: To be added after further
observation of the subject.

"Aunt Emma says I'm supposed to be friends with that boy," I said, nodding toward Tomas. "I'm not very good at making human friends."

"That one?" Bubbles narrowed his eyes at the boy, who was watching us draw closer and closer. "I think he'll work."

"Really? Why?"

"Because you look like you're the same sort of weird. Humans are friends with other humans who are the same sort of weird. Emma is friends with other people who like animals. Callie is friends with other people who annoy me. Yes. He'll work for you. Matching weird."

But Bubbles had to be mistaken. If anything, Tomas looked like he had more in common with Marisol. They were both so *tidy*. Bubbles grumbled in his throat, then dragged me closer.

"Well! Say something to him!" Bubbles growled.

I couldn't believe I was letting myself get ordered around by a Griffin the size of a large toaster, but I asked the boy, "What are you doing?"

"Meeting you to walk around the block," Tomas said.

"No, I mean, why are you standing out here in the street? It's not very safe."

"I have to avoid the marigolds." He pointed at the flowers around his mailbox. "I'm allergic."

"To marigolds?"

"To flowers."

I looked around. A two-second survey confirmed that the neighborhood was full of flowers. "Shouldn't you just stay inside, then? They're everywhere."

"My mom says I need to get some fresh air." He sighed terribly. "She doesn't understand that I'm allergic to air too."

Bubbles abruptly lunged forward.

Tomas let out a sound like a bicycle tire losing pressure and leaped back. But the Griffin wasn't attacking—he was just interested in taking a huge bite of the marigolds. He munched them, staining his beak yellow. Even though he was making little yum-yum sounds as if the flowers were delicious, his face still looked cranky.

"Griffins are hypoallergenic," I offered, because Tomas still looked scared. The *Guide* had a section on pets recommended for people with allergies, and Griffins were in there. Even very sensitive people rarely reacted to Griffin dander. This was important because even though not many people were allergic to magical creatures, the ones who were had rather . . . *magical* reactions.

"Even if they're hypoallergenic, they still bite," Tomas said. "The bacteria in their mouths can take down a full-grown man, you know. And I am not a grown man. And

I'm predisposed to even minor infections. And that Griffin looks like he already wants to bite me."

"That's just the way his face looks," I said, making a mental note to remember that bit about the bacteria in Griffins' mouths so I could add it to the *Guide*. I was pretty impressed that Tomas knew something I didn't know about Griffins. Not many people did.

Tomas suddenly sneezed so hard his hair waved back and forth on his head. He looked at the marigolds accusingly, then said, "Callie told my brothers about you. And they told me. Did you really cause a Unicorn stampede at your school?"

I sighed and said, "Yes." It was easier to say yes than it was to explain everything. Well, maybe not *easier*, since it made me really sad that everyone thought I'd just decided to hop on a Unicorn that day. But at the very least, saying yes made things a lot less complicated.

Tomas asked, "And is the *other* part true too? Do you really think you can talk to magical creatures?" He lifted his eyebrows, which made his glasses slide down his nose.

Well! Tomas got straight to the point, didn't he?

I frowned. "I don't *think* I can do it. It's not pretend. I really can talk to them." I braced myself to be laughed at, or pointed at, or maybe eyebrow-raised at.

Instead, Tomas said, "That's unbelievable."

Before I had time to protest, he added, "I'm allergic to three hundred forty-seven things so far. And I have brittle bones. And my blood doesn't clot right. And I'm prone to concussions. People are always telling me, 'That's *unbelievable*.'"

Bubbles had finished eating the marigolds. He'd left nothing but the little green stubs sticking out of the ground like spikes. I asked Tomas, "Wait, so does that mean you believe me?"

Tomas shrugged. That wasn't a yes, but, for the first time, it also wasn't a no.

Bubbles suddenly tugged at his leash and told me, "I'm done eating. Let's go." He dragged me a few feet. For an old, rickety Griffin the size of a toaster, he was quite strong.

"We're going now? *Right* now?" Tomas asked. He took an inhaler out of his pocket and puffed on it a few times, looking a bit terrified that the moment to leave had finally arrived.

"You don't have to if you're really scared," I said, even though I did want him to come along now. "I could come visit you in your front yard again."

"I never get to do anything," Tomas said. "Everything is too dangerous. All my brothers get to play football, and go to camp, and eat dairy products. I never get to do anything."

So Tomas took one step, then another. Every step we took, Tomas got a little prancier, until finally, about half-way around, he burst out, "I'm walking! I'm walking around a block! I haven't had a migraine or a stomachache or a seizure or reacted badly to the dandelion pollen! We should do it again. Are you going to be here long?"

"All summer," I said.

Bubbles suddenly stopped in his tracks. I accidentally hauled on his leash, and he grumbled, *"Hey!"*

"Sorry," I said. "What are you doing?"

"What?" Tomas asked.

I pointed to the Griffin. "I was asking Bubbles."

Tomas raised his eyebrows but didn't tell me I was being strange. He said, "Carry on."

"Okay, what are you doing?" I asked Bubbles.

"Smelling," he grunted. Hedges lined this part of the sidewalk, and he rooted around in the ivy growing beneath them. "This is weird. Look."

Tomas and I both paused to observe Bubbles as he investigated the ivy. The patch Bubbles sniffed was . . . smoking. The leaves were darkened and curled. It was as if they were trying to catch on fire but were too damp.

I'd never seen burning plants before, but I figured my reaction should be the same as when I saw anything else burning.

In other words, it was time to get a grown-up.

"We need to tell someone," I said. "Even though it's not really on fire, it—"

A thin spray of water interrupted me. It was coming from a large bottle of saline eye drops that Tomas had pulled from his pocket. He squirted the saline solution all over the leaves until they stopped smoking. Then he snapped the top back on and returned it to his pocket.

I was impressed.

"Do you always have that with you?" I asked.

He shrugged. "Pretty much. I might get dry eyes."

We both studied the now-damp leaves. Bubbles, who had gotten saline solution in his ear, looked peevish.

"Why do you think those leaves were smoldering?" I asked. "I didn't see anything that would light them on fire."

"I don't know," Tomas said. "I don't like it, though. Also, if you inhale the smoke of a burning poison ivy plant, you can get a rash in your lungs."

I found a stick and poked the ground. "This isn't poison ivy."

"I *know*. I was just telling you that if it *was*."

I tapped my chin. "I think this is interesting, Tomas. I like interesting things."

Tomas hurried to catch up with me as I started to walk again. He said, "I'm pretty sure I'm allergic to interesting things."

CHAPTER
— 3 —

Sometimes Things Catch Fire

By the time I'd been in Cloverton for two days, I knew the routine: Wake up early, eat fast, and then get to the clinic to prepare for the parade of patients. I was thrilled that Aunt Emma trusted me with small tasks, even though the tasks themselves weren't very thrilling.

Here is a short list of things I had to do:

1. Remove the poop pellets from the Two-Horned Pawpigs' enclosures.
2. Make sure the Glowing Nectarbirds had plenty of spiderwebs in their cages.
3. Dig up one hundred roly-poly bugs from the backyard so Aunt Emma could make a remedy from them.

(I thought the illness probably had to be pretty bad if taking a medicine made of roly-poly bugs was better.)

The plus side was that I was learning things I couldn't learn from the *Guide*. I figured Jeffrey Higgleston would have been very impressed with all the firsthand experience I was getting. He would have called it *fieldwork*.

On this particular afternoon, Aunt Emma found me doing my fieldwork in the large animal stable, observing the Standard Griffins as they ate. (Did you know they are the only breed of Griffin with teeth as well as beaks? Now you do.)

"Would you like to come with me on a house call at the end of the day?" Aunt Emma asked.

We both knew what my answer would be.

"Can we bring Tomas?" I asked.

Aunt Emma looked pleased that she'd chosen such a good friend for me. "He can come if his parents say it's okay," she told me. "And if he brings his inhaler."

A half hour later, Tomas, Aunt Emma, and I arrived at a bright white house with spiral-shaped plants on either side of the door. Everything about it looked crisp and clean, like a magazine house. It reminded me a little of my grandmother's house—the grandmother who liked to be called Grandmoney—which meant it was probably a place where people would tell me not to leave fingerprints on the wall. To my relief, Aunt Emma led us around to the back-yard without knocking on the house's door.

"Why doesn't the owner just bring his pet to the clinic?" Tomas asked.

"Regent Maximus can be tricky," Aunt Emma answered over her shoulder, shifting her heavy bag from one hand to the other. "He's a bit timid."

I suddenly noticed we were walking toward a small stable painted to match the house. Was Regent Maximus a standard Griffin? A Pegasus? Surely not—

"A Unicorn!" Tomas said when Aunt Emma slid the stable door open.

My stomach flip-flopped. Unicorns! Me! What was Aunt Emma thinking?

I hadn't seen a Unicorn in person since the Unicorn Incident, and to be honest, I didn't really want to see one again for a long time. I still thought they were beautiful and impressive, but I hadn't come *close* to forgetting how they were also show-offs and bad listeners and careless around breakable geodes.

"I should stay out here," Tomas said. "I'm *really* allergic to Unicorns."

"Maybe I should stay with you," I said slowly.

"I'll be okay," Tomas said, totally missing the *no-I-want-to-stay-here* look I was giving him.

"No, Pip, you should see this," Aunt Emma said. "It's your sort of thing! Come on!" Before I could come up with

Unicorn

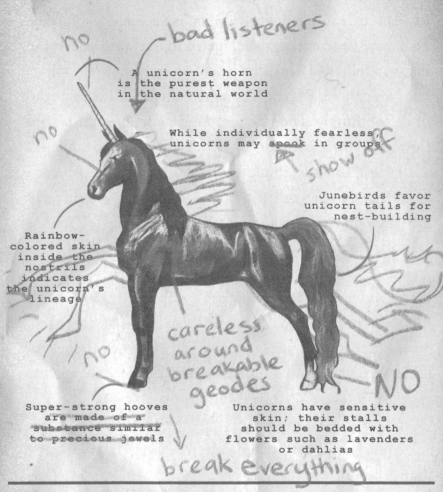

no — bad listeners

no

A unicorn's horn is the purest weapon in the natural world

While individually fearless, unicorns may spook in groups

show off

Junebirds favor unicorn tails for nest-building

Rainbow-colored skin inside the nostrils indicates the unicorn's lineage

no

careless around breakable geodes

NO

Super-strong hooves are made of a substance similar to precious jewels

Unicorns have sensitive skin; their stalls should be bedded with flowers such as lavenders or dahlias

break everything

SIZE: 30–80"
WEIGHT: 400–3,200 lbs.
DESCRIPTION: Of all of the magical animals, the Unicorn is the most famous, and rightly so. This noble and bold creature comes in all shapes and colors, boasts populations on every continent, and has been the stuff of legend for centuries. These vibrant companions are prized for their looks and

an excuse, she motioned for me to follow her. I didn't want to seem scared, and if Aunt Emma had somehow forgotten about the Unicorn Incident, then I didn't want to remind her, so I followed her in.

"Hey there, Regent Maximus!" my aunt called ahead of us soothingly. The stable around us smelled dusty and flowery, like old potpourri. "How's my pretty boy doing?"

I snorted a little, thinking about how much the Unicorn would love to be called pretty. I certainly wouldn't tell him, though. No, I was going to pretend I couldn't understand a thing this Unicorn was saying! Mom was always telling me that mistakes are learning experiences, and I'd definitely learned that talking to Unicorns was a *very* bad—

"*You're coming to hurt me!*" the Unicorn screeched.

Both my aunt and I jumped. The Unicorn dashed to the corner of his stall and fell down into the honeysuckle and lavender hay, shivering.

My heart was still racing. "A *little* timid?" I asked.

Aunt Emma put her hand on her chest. "Maybe more than a little."

"Are you okay?" Tomas called from the stable door. "Be careful! Unicorn horn wounds are hard to stitch shut. You could bleed out in seconds. I only brought one box of bandages!"

"We're fine, Tomas!" I said. Well, Aunt Emma and I

were fine. Regent Maximus was now frantically burying his head in the hay. I frowned. I really, really wanted to assure the Unicorn that we weren't coming to hurt him, but I kept my lips sealed.

"Is that you, Emma?" a deep voice called out from the front of the stable. A man in a suit was walking up behind Tomas. He looked like the house: crisp and clean and straight-lined.

"Good evening, Bill!" Aunt Emma said brightly. "I thought you'd still be overseas! When did you get back?"

"Earlier today," the man said. He eyed Tomas and me, possibly thinking about the greasy fingerprints we might leave.

"My niece Pip and her friend Tomas," Aunt Emma explained, motioning to each of us in turn. "They're helping me out. Pip and Tomas, this is Mr. Henshaw."

"I see!" Mr. Henshaw said. "You're giving him his monthly Pixieworm pill, right? How's it coming?"

"He hasn't gored them yet," Tomas said from the stable door. He clutched a pack of tissues in one hand and a bottle of nose spray in the other. For all his talk of allergies and the world wanting to kill him, I hadn't seen any evidence of a reaction in the two days we'd spent together. I was relieved. Now that I'd gotten used to talking with him, I really liked Tomas.

"He wasn't going to gore us," I said quickly. "But I didn't expect him to be so . . . shy."

"Yes, well . . ." Mr. Henshaw rubbed his temples. "Regent Maximus is supposed to be a show Unicorn, you know. His full name is Multicolored Lies the Head That Wears the Crown. He was terribly expensive."

"I suppose not everyone's cut out for show business," Aunt Emma said, rummaging in her bag. She retrieved a bottle with a single pill in the bottom. Regent Maximus, who had pulled his head out of the hay, watched her warily from the back of the stall. His rainbow-colored mane was tangled with bedding and stuck up all over. He looked nothing at all like the Barreras' Unicorns.

Aunt Emma went on. "Do you have an apple? Or even better, a piece of honeycomb? Something I can lure him forward with? We could force him to take this, but I think it will be better in the long run if we can show him it's not such a hard process."

"I'm not certain what he'll like—shall we go take a look?" Mr. Henshaw motioned toward his house.

"Sure!" said Aunt Emma. "Pip, Tomas, why don't you wait here and try to get him used to people being in the stable."

"Is that really a good idea?" I asked.

"Just no Unicorn rides," she said, winking at me. So

she hadn't forgotten! She just trusted me, which felt pretty excellent. I nodded, and she disappeared with Mr. Henshaw.

"Woe! Woe, woe, woe! They're going to hurt me!" Regent Maximus muttered from his stall. "Oh! Wait! They've left! I'm saved!"

I folded my arms. I was *not* talking to this Unicorn.

"Oh, no! The small ones are left! They're probably the most dangerous." The top of Regent Maximus's head poked up over the top of the stall. His watery eyes regarded me, wide and fearful. "I bet that one's going to eat me."

"I am not going to eat you!" I said before I thought better of it.

Now Regent Maximus's eyes went *really* wide. "You can understand me and talk to me!"

I sighed. "I *can*, but I'm trying not to."

"Because you're going to eat me, and you don't want to get friendly!"

"I'm not going to eat you!"

Tomas leaned into the stable. "Pip, are you talking to that Unicorn?"

I started, "I am—"

"You *are* going to eat me!" Regent Maximus wailed.

"Wait, no, I was talking to Tomas!" I said, but it was no use—Regent Maximus was now desperately pawing at the outside door of his stall, trying to escape. The wood began to splinter.

He was just as dramatic as the other Unicorns. But as mad as I was about Unicorns in general, I had to admit, I felt pretty bad for Regent Maximus. It's never fun to be scared.

"Is he charging?" Tomas yelled. "I'll never survive if he charges! My blood clots slowly!"

"Now the shiny boy is yelling at me! It's a battle cry! Save me!" Regent Maximus cried out the stall's tiny window. "Can anyone hear me? They're here to eat me—"

"Both of you, stop!" I finally shouted, loud enough that a wild Nectarbird in the rafters flapped off, muttering angrily. Tomas and Regent Maximus fell silent. I took a deep breath. "Regent Maximus, neither of us is going to eat you—do you really think we could eat a full-grown Unicorn? And, Tomas, Regent Maximus is *not* charging. Everyone got it?"

Both of them gazed at me suspiciously.

In a very, very low voice, Regent Maximus whispered out of the side of his mouth, "If that boy doesn't want to eat me, then why is he lurking in the shadows?"

This wasn't exactly true—Tomas stood in full sunlight, and technically, the Unicorn was the one lurking in shadows—but I could see why it might make him nervous.

I asked, "Tomas, would you come say hi to him? He thinks you don't like him."

"I like him. I just don't want to die," Tomas said, but he walked forward anyway. He had barely taken a step when he began to sneeze.

"Wow, you really are especially allergic to Unicorns," I said.

"That's just the lavender," Tomas said, only now his nose was all stuffy, so it sounded like "Has hus he lavender." Because Regent Maximus wouldn't understand Tomas if he actually said hello, Tomas waved a bit.

"See, Regent Maximus? We're not scary," I said. I picked up the pill bottle and shook out the single pill, which was bright blue. "So, look: All Aunt Emma wants is for you to take this pill."

"It's *blue*," the Unicorn whimpered.

"Yes," I agreed. "Isn't that pretty? It will keep you from getting Pixieworms. Trust me, you don't want to get Pixieworms . . . they burrow in your . . . well, never mind. They're just not something you want."

Regent Maximus flicked his ears back and forth anxiously. "Are you going to stuff it down my throat?"

"I really don't want to," I answered. "If you just swallow it, it'll be over in a second."

The Unicorn considered. He stamped his foot. For a moment, I thought nothing would happen. But then he stretched his neck out long, so he didn't have to actually move any closer. His nose made it over the side of the stall, toward me.

"Careful, Pip," Tomas said softly, with a nervous look at Regent Maximus's horn. It was shinier and longer than Fortnight's had been, which made me feel rather smug on Regent Maximus's behalf. The Unicorn dipped his head, pressed his muzzle into my hand, and ate the pill in one loud crunch.

"There!" I exclaimed. "See? Was that so bad?"

"Yes," Tomas said, in a sort of strangled voice. He gave a loud, strange hiccup. And as he hiccuped, a bright green bubble came out of his mouth.

"Whoa!" I said. "How'd you do that?"

"I (*hic*—purple bubble) told you (*hic*—fuchsia bubble) I was especially (*hic*—blue bubble) allergic to Unicorns. This is what happens!"

Like I said before, magical creature allergies are pretty rare. I'd never known anyone who had them before. So even though I knew the reactions were supposed to be very unusual, I was amazed by just how very unusual this reaction was.

"Will you be okay?" I asked.

Tomas looked cross. "If you call *this* okay!"

He hiccuped a bunch of times in a row, so that the whole stable was full of multicolored bubbles. They bounced around, eventually popping when they knocked against the ceiling.

Even Regent Maximus laughed. Nervously, but still. It was something.

"They will stop, right?" I asked.

Tomas hiccuped a sunshine-yellow bubble. "Eventual—" The last syllable of the word was lost as a pink bubble erupted.

I suddenly grinned at him. "Isn't this great? I mean, aside from the bubbles? We helped a Unicorn!"

I saw Tomas's answering smile through a large yellow bubble.

"Hey—what's that smell?" Tomas asked in between hiccups (an orange bubble and another yellow one). I sniffed the air. Something *did* smell strange. I frowned, and scanned the stable. All three of us saw it at once.

Smoke.

Coming from the last stall in the stable, a thick plume of black smoke curled toward the ceiling.

"Fire!" Regent Maximus and Tomas yelled at nearly the same moment.

This time, it was too much to handle with a bottle of eye drops.

"Quick!" I shouted at Tomas. "Help me with this!" He hurried to help me grab the handle of Regent Maximus's water bucket. We staggered toward the smoke.

Flames already filled the unoccupied stall, climbing hungrily toward the ceiling. When we hurled the contents of the bucket at the fire, it just hissed. Steam rolled out at us, pushing multicolored bubbles up to the ceiling. It'd take way more than a little water to put this out. The smoke burned my eyes.

"Tomas, go get Aunt Emma!" I had to yell to be heard over the crackly sound of fire eating up wood. As Tomas bolted out of the stable, I grabbed a silver Unicorn halter from the hook beside Regent Maximus's stall. "Regent Maximus, are you listening to me? Let's get you out of here."

The Unicorn thrashed around his stall, crazy with terror. His horn looked especially scary in the firelight. I couldn't open the door—I was afraid he'd charge forward without listening, just like the Barreras' Unicorns. The fire was getting worse. Spare bits of burning lavender floated through the air. There wasn't much time.

Leaning over the stall door, I grabbed hold of his horn, then yanked his face down toward me. "Regent Maximus!

Stop it! It's time to be brave! Don't panic, and stay close!" I used my best Callie voice, since people don't mess around with Callie, and it worked. Regent Maximus still stamped and shied and whinnied worriedly, but I got the halter on. Holding the lead tight, I opened the stall door, and the two of us ran outside into the fresh air.

Tomas's bubbles were still floating up into the clouds above us.

Regent Maximus reared, and I dangled at the end of the lead. My stomach felt like it was in a washing machine. He whinnied, and it just meant this: "Aaaaaaaaaaaaaaah!" I wouldn't be able to hold on to the halter much longer.

"Pip! We're coming!" Tomas shouted. He was running from the house, inhaler in his hand. Aunt Emma was close behind him with a big fire extinguisher, and Mr. Henshaw was just behind her.

"I've got the Unicorn," Mr. Henshaw said to my aunt as Regent Maximus returned his front feet and my regular feet to the ground. "Get the fire!" Aunt Emma rushed right past me, into the stable. There was a loud hissing sound. The smoke turned white.

Mr. Henshaw took Regent Maximus's lead from me. As he led the Unicorn over to a little riding ring and locked him inside, I sat down on the grass and tried to breathe slowly. I felt all wobbly. Tomas sat beside me and offered me his inhaler. When I shook my head, he patted my shoulder awkwardly instead.

As Mr. Henshaw returned to us, Aunt Emma emerged from the stable. Her face was all sooty, but other than that she looked okay. Her expression was tight, though.

"Close one," she coughed. "Everyone fine?"

"Yes," I said, and then something occurred to me: Based on my track record of magical-creature-related catastrophes, it was very likely this would all get blamed on me.

I suddenly felt like I had Pixieworms in my stomach.

"It started out of nowhere!" I protested. "Ask Tomas! I promise, Aunt Emma, this wasn't like at the school. Tomas and I were just standing there and suddenly—"

"Pip, calm down," Aunt Emma said. She wiped her forehead with the crook of her arm. It mostly just smeared the soot around. "I know it wasn't you."

"What was it?" Tomas asked. "What started the fire?"

Aunt Emma grimaced before holding out her hand. In her palm was a fat ball of fur that was once gray but was now mostly white, covered with fire extinguisher dust. Suddenly, two giant, watery eyes opened near the center of the fur ball, watching me carefully.

I had no idea what the creature was.

Aunt Emma gave the blinking animal a dark look and said, "It was Fuzzles."

CHAPTER
4

Fuzzles Make Terrible Pets

The first thing I did when I got back home that evening was help Aunt Emma set up Regent Maximus in the large animal stable—he'd be staying with us until Mr. Henshaw got his burned-up one fixed. It took ages, because Regent Maximus was sure he would fall and drown in the water trough, or get bitten by lavender mites, or stab himself with his own horn.

"Couldn't you have stabbed yourself just as easily back home, though?" I said to him, whispering so Aunt Emma wouldn't catch me talking to a Unicorn.

"*You're right!* Oh, oh! I've been living so *recklessly*!" Regent Maximus wailed into the stable rafters.

The *second* thing I did when I got back home was gallop upstairs for *Jeffrey Higgleston's Guide to Magical Creatures*.

Fuzzles. Fuzzles. Fuzzles.

Why couldn't I remember what the *Guide* had said about them?

When I flipped open the *Guide* to their page, I understood why. It barely said anything at all.

You'd think an animal that turns into a fireball would deserve more description.

I charged back downstairs. Callie was sitting on the arm of the sofa, painting her toenails the color of unripe tomatoes and making vowel sounds. She did this in the mornings sometimes too. She'd told me this was to "exercise her voice" for "clarity onstage."

In the cluttered kitchen area, Aunt Emma held her phone to her ear and paced. "Only one at the moment," she told the phone in a serious voice. "Yes, yes, we have it contained." We all looked to the round kitchen table. A metal box containing the Fuzzle sat in the middle. A small curl of smoke trailed from one of the breathing holes.

Aunt Emma hung up, sighed, and ran her hand through her hair. "Callie, I'm sorry, but I can't take you to the movie tonight."

Callie started to leap up before remembering her wet toenails. Instead, she merely pushed herself up on her elbows with as much anger as possible. "*What?!* I've hardly gone out all *summer*."

Fuzzle

DESCRIPTION: Pest.

"That's not true!" Aunt Emma said, sounding a little offended. "I took you to the fabric store last week to get sequins for that . . . that mermaid costume thing."

"That was three weeks ago, Mom. And it was a siren costume. Mermaids are for, like, kids. Delynn and I are trying to convince the school to do a musical version of *The Odyssey*. It would be incredible."

Aunt Emma made a face that told me she realized Callie was right about the timing.

"I'll make it up to you, Callie. Anything you want. But right now I need to look under the crawl space to make sure there aren't any Fuzzles down there. This house is very old and I don't trust the smoke detectors."

"This is ridiculous," Callie muttered. "I am persecuted."

"We're all persecuted," Aunt Emma replied. "I'm hoping this is a one-off incident and we won't find any more in Cloverton. Come on, you can hold the flashlight for me. Maybe that Doxel still lives down there!"

Callie's eyes widened with obvious distaste. Her left eye widened more than the other. Like this: O.o.

I guess she didn't care for Doxels.

"I'll help!" I said eagerly.

"She speaks!" Callie snorted.

"Callie!" Aunt Emma chastised. "Say sorry. *Now*."

"Sorry, *now*," Callie said. "I guess I'll order pizza. Again." With a meaningful look at her mother, she turned to me. "What would *you* like on it, Pip?"

I was so glad to be asked, even if it was just to show Aunt Emma she was being nice to me. I said happily, "Oh, it doesn't matter. I only eat the crust anyway."

"Get me some with pineapple," grumbled Bubbles. I hadn't even noticed him lying on top of the living room bookshelf. He had wedged himself in between one of Aunt Emma's wedding photographs and a trophy in the shape of four horned birds. He did so hate it when Callie sang.

"I mean, I like pineapple on mine," I said quickly. I wanted to get on Bubbles's good side. "They have that, right?"

"Weirdo," Callie muttered. But she jotted it down on a notepad.

Ten minutes later, Aunt Emma and I were crouched in the dirty space beneath the house. It was nothing but brick rubble and dirt for the floor and concrete blocks for the too-close walls. Oh, and some spiders (zero Doxels). It was a very not-Callie kind of place. Aunt Emma poked the nozzle of the fire extinguisher in a corner while I played the flashlight beam over the top of it.

"Aunt Emma?" I asked. "Can I ask you a question?"

My aunt spun around to face me, eyes wide with concern. "Of course, Pip! Is everything all right?"

"It's just that I looked in the *Guide* for Fuzzles, and it barely says anything at all. Can you believe that? Why wouldn't there be more about them in there?"

Aunt Emma smiled at me and spoke with obvious relief in her voice. "Well, the *Guide* really focuses on animals rather than pests. Fuzzles are more like insects than creatures, really. And they're not all *that* common. Thankfully."

"*Thankfully*, because they burn down stables?"

"Exactly," Aunt Emma said. "When they get surprised or scared, Fuzzles catch fire. It doesn't hurt *them*, but it hurts pretty much everything else."

She paused.

"Also, um, they have litters of three hundred FuzzleKits every three weeks during the summer."

I did the math in my head.

"Oh my gosh," I said. "That's why you hope the Fuzzle from the barn is the only one!"

"Exactly."

Now I too was hoping the Fuzzle in the box was the only one. I was also kind of hoping to get a better look at it. Because I didn't think it mattered if Fuzzles were pests. They still deserved a better entry in the *Guide*. They were fascinating!

Overhead, we heard the pizza delivery person come and go. Callie shouted, "*MOM! PIZZA! OH, YEAH, PIP TOO! PIZZA!*"

We poked around for a few more minutes before Aunt Emma said, "It looks pretty clear down here. I don't see any signs of nests or warrens. Fingers crossed it really was just one Fuzzle who lost its way."

But it wasn't.

"So then *he* said that she didn't have the stage presence to pull off the role, and *she* said that *he* wouldn't know— what? Yes, I'm talking about him! No, not the guy who originated the part, the second one—yes—" Callie was on the phone. I wondered if whoever was on the other end of the line understood Callie. I sure didn't.

I sat at a table just over Callie's shoulder, studying the Fuzzle. It was still contained in the little metal box, and had rolled itself over to a tiny water dish I put inside.

Even though it was a pest, I didn't think it should go thirsty.

I'd gone through all Aunt Emma's old magical veterinary school textbooks looking for information on Fuzzles, and hadn't found a single sentence. I peered into the box and doodled some flames on the back of my hand.

"Hey, Fuzzle?" I whispered. "Come on. Talk to me! Why are you here?"

The Fuzzle didn't answer. It just blinked at me, grumbled a bit, and then hummed. It sounded like this: *grrrrrrrrrrrrr mmmmmmmmmmmm*. Except the "m" went on forever and ever and ever, until I gave up. I couldn't tell if the Fuzzles didn't *want* to talk to me or simply *couldn't*. They didn't really seem to have mouths, after all.

"Did I just hear you talk to that thing? Because you know you're not supposed to pretend you can talk to animals anymore," Callie said, crossing her arms. She'd hung up and was now standing over me. She narrowed her eyes at both me and the Fuzzle, who was rolling itself back and forth happily. It was pretty cute for something that turned into a miniature inferno.

"I was talking to myself," I said, which wasn't entirely untrue, seeing as how the Fuzzle hadn't answered. Catching a glimpse of the old, sticker-covered computer at the front desk, I suddenly had an idea. "Do you think I could use the computer?"

"Ha!" Callie said. "Mom has that thing so locked down with parental controls that it's cruel and unusual punishment. She says—"

"That the computer is just for work," Aunt Emma finished the sentence, suddenly rounding the corner. She was holding a Jillymander by the tail. I didn't think I'd like to be hung upside down, but the Jillymander was purring, so I guessed it was fine. She added, "Don't roll your eyes at me, Callie. You're on the computer plenty enough during the school year. It's summer! Get out! Explore!"

"By *explore*, do you mean the vast, uncharted terrain of the front desk?" Callie asked, crossing her arms.

"Well . . . explore after hours, then," Aunt Emma said, but I could tell she felt a little bad. She and the Jillymander vanished into an exam room just as the phone rang. Callie lunged for it.

"Delynn? Did you watch the audition video? What? This isn't Delynn? Yes, this is Cloverton Clinic for Magical Creatures. What? How is that our problem? No, we don't treat them. Because they're . . . they're Fuzzles! We treat pets, not pests!"

It was the first Fuzzle call. The first of many.

By the time I'd fed Regent Maximus his lunch and taken Bubbles for a walk with Tomas, Callie had received fifty-seven Fuzzle-related phone calls.

"It hasn't stopped ringing!" she said shrilly when

Tomas, Bubbles, and I walked back in the front door. Callie pointed at the phone like it had bitten her. It rang again in response.

Fifty-*eight* Fuzzle-related phone calls.

"Aunt Emma said they can produce three hundred FuzzleKits a week," I told Tomas. "I guess that means the one in Regent Maximus's stable wasn't a stray."

"Three hundred Fuzzles?" Tomas rubbed his nose, as if already imagining an allergic reaction. "That's a lot of fur."

We turned to look as a fire truck whizzed past the clinic, lights flashing and sirens loud.

"That's a lot of *fire*," I added. "I wonder why the Fuzzles showed up all of a sudden? Aunt Emma said they're usually very rare."

But by closing time, Fuzzles were no longer very rare— or, at least, they were no longer very rare at Cloverton Clinic for Magical Creatures.

It turned out that no one in Cloverton knew what to *do* with the Fuzzles. The police suggested quarantining them in fireproof boxes, but no one had enough lying around. The fire department suggested dousing the Fuzzles in water so they'd burn slower, but that just created a lot of steam before the inevitable fire. Cloverton Animal Control didn't know what to do with them, so they kept sending calls to us.

At three o'clock, Aunt Emma suggested Callie simply take the phone off the hook. And it worked!

For about thirty minutes, anyway. When people didn't get an answer, they stopped calling and started showing up at the door with Fuzzles. Fuzzles in metal lock boxes. Fuzzles in empty coffee tins. Fuzzles in jelly jars. Fuzzles on glass cake platters, and even a few Fuzzles wrapped in tin foil like fuzzy baked potatoes.

Aunt Emma and Callie ran to the store to buy more fire extinguishers. Tomas and I were charged with keeping the waiting room from burning down.

"This is ridiculous!" Tomas said, throwing his hands in the air. I wasn't sure what Tomas meant was ridiculous—the hundreds of Fuzzles or the big puffs of periwinkle-colored smoke that were coming out of his ears. I was beginning to think Tomas really *was* allergic to all magical creatures.

I stood on the desk, holding a fire extinguisher. Every now and then, a Fuzzle would smoke, and I'd spray it down. It was working for now, but what were we supposed to do overnight? Take shifts?

"Incoming," Tomas warned as a car rolled up outside.

The driver hopped out, ran to the front door, dropped a metal trash can full of Fuzzles on the doorstep, then squealed off.

Not very noble.

"Pip! Quick!" Tomas said. He pointed to a Fuzzle off to his left that was smoking. I aimed the fire extinguisher at it and blasted, but the spray didn't quite reach. The smoke deepened in color.

"Hurry!" Tomas said as I jumped off the counter and tiptoed through the sea of Fuzzles on the floor. I wasn't going to make it in time! Tomas flung himself forward. He grabbed for the smoking Fuzzle, but he couldn't quite reach. Fingers stretched, he grasped, his fingertips scratching across the Fuzzle's blond fur—

The Fuzzle stopped smoking.

Tomas and I exchanged a puzzled look.

I wound my way over. "What did you do?"

"Nothing," Tomas said. "I just—I guess I just sort of . . ." Reaching forward again, he scratched the Fuzzle on its head.

The Fuzzle opened its eyes and looked up at Tomas happily. It began to trill. Like when you roll your tongue and sort of sing. That's what the Fuzzle sounded like. It trilled faster and faster until the sound just became a hum.

And then the humming was everywhere. All the other Fuzzles in the waiting room were harmonizing with the first.

And better yet? They'd *all* stopped smoking. Well, except for Tomas. Puffs of allergic smoke still trailed from his ears.

With a sigh of relief, I set the fire extinguisher down. "Well. *That's* definitely something about Fuzzles that belongs in the *Guide*."

"But what about all the others?" Tomas said. "I mean, the ones out there?" He waved toward the front door and beyond. "People can't go around petting Fuzzles all day."

"No," I agreed. "But at least we won't be stuck in another burning building."

Tomas nodded and scratched the Fuzzle's head a little harder.

That night, after we'd sorted the Fuzzles into fireproof containers and double-checked the smoke detectors, I fell happily into my bed. I was almost asleep when someone opened my bedroom door. The silhouette looked like a gangly monster topped with a mushroom of fur. I sat up, confused, and realized it was Callie. She wore pink pajamas and her hair was all piled on top of her head.

I didn't say anything. I just stared at her and thought about her looking like a monster with mushroom hair.

"Look," Callie said. "Stop staring at me like that. I don't really get this whole magical-creature-guide-knowledge-memorizing thing you do, but fine, whatever, because I want these Fuzzles g-o-n-e, *gone*."

I knew she'd told me to stop staring, but I couldn't think of any other response.

Callie reached down and turned my head to the side, so my eyes were pointed at the wall. "Just tell me—what do you need to know about them to make them go away?"

To the wall, I said, "I've already gone through the *Guide*—"

"I mean, what can I find for you on the . . ." Callie dropped her voice. "Computer?"

I turned back to face her. "What about the parental controls?"

"Please," Callie said, looking smug. "I'm good for more than just a flawless line-by-line recitation of *Romeo and Juliet*. You really think I'd sit up there all day without the Internet?"

The world suddenly opened up. Surely someone else had to know something more about Fuzzles, and surely that someone else had put it on a website.

"Oh. Well . . . anything. Anything you can find out would help. Like, habitat. That means where they live."

"I know what *habitat* means," Callie said scornfully. "Right. I'll see what I can do."

The next day, I discovered there was a lot more to Fuzzles than I'd thought.

CHAPTER
— 5 —

Check Your Underwear

The next day started with a scream. It was Callie, and it was not the scary kind of scream that would make you jump up from your breakfast. Instead, it was the kind that made me and Aunt Emma look at each other over the kitchen table. Aunt Emma's eyes narrowed, and then she took another bite of her still-frozen toaster waffle. I drank my juice.

A moment later, Callie stomped in. The ends of her hair were smoking. She held up a metal wastebasket that I recognized from her bedroom: It had pink flowers decaled on the side. Well, it *previously* had. Most of the decals were now melted off. More smoke erupted from the top of it.

"I found another one!" Callie said, frenzied. "In my underwear drawer!"

Aunt Emma looked sympathetic. "It must have come looking for the ones in the clinic. Fuzzles lump together, you know."

"Well, they're not allowed to lump together *in my underwear*!" Callie slammed the wastebasket on the table. "Can't we get rid of them?"

"Callie, no trash cans on the table," Aunt Emma said. "And I'm trying to think of a way to move them safely, but it's tricky since everyone thinks of them as pests. I'll need to rearrange some of my appointments to this afternoon, I think." She gestured to the Fuzzle in the trash can. It was blinking at Callie. "Do you think you can take care of that one?"

"One! One?" Callie echoed. She sounded a little unhinged. "Did you see what I took care of in the clinic yesterday? Millions! What's one more! One! One!"

I had seen Callie melt down on two family occasions before, and neither time had been pretty. I definitely didn't want to be standing in such close range. Turning to my aunt, I asked quickly, "Can I go over to Tomas's house? I want to talk to him about the Fuzzles."

"A brainstorm session?" Aunt Emma replied with a smile.

I smiled back. "Yeah."

"That's a great idea, Pip. Cloverton certainly could use all the Fuzzle help it can get."

"Oh, please," Callie said, slamming the trash can around a little bit. "How about instead of brainstorming, we all go to the mall to buy me some new underwear? *Oh, wait*, we can't, because then no one would be here to protect us from *exploding furballs*!"

I hardly considered what the Fuzzles did to be *exploding*, but I certainly wasn't going to say that out loud. I didn't want Callie mad at me ever, and I definitely didn't want her mad at me today, since I needed her help with the Fuzzle research. Getting up from the table, I took my plate to the sink. Callie folded her arms and gave the Fuzzle a look that should have made it catch fire again.

"You little beast," Callie said. "This is the worst summer I've ever had! I wish I lived with—with—dentists!"

"Now, Callie—" Aunt Emma started.

I hustled outside before I heard any more. As I made my way down the sidewalk to Tomas's house, I hoped he wasn't busy—I hadn't gone over without calling before. It was hard to imagine him having hobbies, but it was possible that his family might have decided to go somewhere for the day.

I quickly realized that at least a few of the Ramirezes were home, because as I knocked on the door, I heard shouting.

One voice, sort of older and boyish and nervous-making, shouted, "I *didn't* put it in there!"

"Jorges?" This was an older voice, sort of mom-like.

"It wasn't me!"

She shot out again. "Eric? I know it was you!"

Tomas's voice wailed out, high and reedy, "Eric's at Asia's house!"

"Fuzzles don't just appear in my underwear—"

The door still hadn't been answered. I noticed a doorbell and rang it. The door opened nearly at once, and Tomas stood on the other side with a Band-Aid on his forehead. The walls on either side of him were covered with one thousand little pottery things. Plates and stars and beads.

"What happened to your head?" I asked. "An allergic reaction?"

"I hit it on the fridge," Tomas replied. "I was trying to get away from the cheese."

"Let me guess—you're allergic to cheese."

He nodded grimly. Behind him, I saw two biggish boys gallop across the hall, laughing furiously. A voice—it had to be Ms. Ramirez—howled, "You boys come right back here and take care of this thing!"

Tomas glanced furtively over his shoulder. "Mom found a Fuzzle in her underwear drawer this morning. She thinks one of my brothers did it."

"Callie found one in *her* underwear drawer!" I exclaimed. "Aunt Emma said they like to lump together, but maybe they also like tiny spaces. Or underwear."

"Then my bedroom should be full of them," Tomas replied darkly.

"Because you have a lot of underwear?" I asked, confused.

"No, because I'm the youngest, so my room is the small—"

Ms. Ramirez appeared behind him then, and he went quiet. She was short and plump. Her hair was in ringlets like Raindancer's. A smoking Fuzzle dangled from her thumb and forefinger. "Tomas! Were you born in a gas station? Ask her in."

"Get in," Tomas said, stepping back to let me in.

"That is not any better," Ms. Ramirez said. "You must be Pip. Lovely to meet you."

I was just trying to figure out what to say back when the Fuzzle in her hand burst into flame. Without any fuss or panic, she smacked it against a bare spot on the wall to put out the fire.

"No, Mom!" Tomas said. "Tickle it! You've got to tickle it."

"I would just as soon tickle a rat," Ms. Ramirez replied, looking disgusted. "Pip, your aunt is taking these things in, right?"

"Um," I replied, then "um" again because I wasn't sure I knew how to talk to Ms. Ramirez. I looked at Tomas, who shrugged encouragingly, and finally I said, "Yes, she's taking them in. Sort of."

Ms. Ramirez started down the hall. "Good. Tomas, you need to get some sun, anyway. I'm going to get you a pot or something for you to carry this over to the clinic. Don't drop it! We haven't had much rain and I don't want you to burn down the neighborhood. *JORGES, GET OVER HERE NOW. FIND ME A POT FOR THIS THING.*"

Then she vanished into another room. One of the big boys—Jorges, maybe?—galloped past again, looking like a giant, muscled version of Tomas. Then another boy came, who looked exactly the same, and then another, until I started to feel like I was watching the same part of a movie over and over.

"Oh! Your brothers are triplets!" I realized. "That's so cool."

"Cool if you're a triplet," Tomas replied. "*They* get to do whatever they want. *They* are tall enough to reach whatever they want to reach. *They* don't have allergies."

I could tell he was feeling low about it, so I said, "*They* also don't get to have adventures with Pip Bartlett."

He smiled gloomily at me. Ms. Ramirez reappeared with a large nonstick saucepan. She'd put a glass lid on it, and we could see the Fuzzle crouched in the bottom.

Crouched? Sitting. Lying. Piled. It was hard to tell since it didn't have any legs.

"You bring that pot back," Ms. Ramirez warned Tomas. "I do my pork in that one."

As we stepped outside, I said to Tomas, "Don't you think it's funny that there were Fuzzles in two underwear drawers? Maybe we should ask some of the neighbors if they have found Fuzzles there too! Or at least warn them to protect their underwear."

Tomas rubbed his neck. "I dunno. That sounds kinda . . . awkward."

"But imagine how happy people will be to not have their underwear go up in flames! Plus it'll be safer for the Fuzzles if we collect them all in one spot—they like to lump together, you know," I said, repeating what Aunt Emma told me that morning as if I'd known it all along.

Tomas sighed noisily. "Okay, but I'm not asking."

"I'm not asking!"

"*I'm* not asking. You're the one who keeps saying *underwear*."

We decided to draw up a flyer, since neither of us would ask. It only took a minute, long enough for the Fuzzle to travel around the inside of the saucepan twice, and when we were done, it seemed like it would do most of the explaining for us.

SAVE YOUR UNDERWEAR

Cloverton is experiencing a high volume of fuzzles

They might be nesting in your underwear drawer and they could CATCH FIRE

Please take a moment to check!!!!!

Armed with the flyer and the giant saucepan, we traveled to the next-door neighbor's and knocked on the door. Tomas mistrustfully eyed a bug next to the porch light until the door opened, and then he handed the old woman on the other side the flyer.

"Tomas Ramirez," she said. "What is this nonsense?"

"It's not nonsense," I insisted. I felt particularly brave about talking at the moment, since I knew helping with the Fuzzles was the right thing to do. Plus, the flyer had started the conversation for me. I continued, "You should check your drawer. We're trying to help."

She narrowed her eyes at us for a long moment, and then she turned away, leaving the door open. She stumped out of sight.

"She thinks it's a trick," I told Tomas.

He removed a marker from one of his pockets and wrote THIS IS NOT A TRICK on the bottom of the flyer.

The woman returned. She was holding an enormous pair of flowered underwear. Tomas flinched.

"You were right!" she exclaimed. "There were two of them in there! I'm not touching them. Here, take all of it!"

Tomas was still staring at the underwear with wide eyes, so I snatched off the pot lid. She dropped the underwear inside; it landed with a soft thud. I guessed that was because of the Fuzzles inside it.

"I don't need those back," she said. "Tell your mother hello, Tomas."

She shut the door.

"I don't believe it!" Tomas peered into the pot with his head turned sideways, like he couldn't look at the underwear straight on.

"Let's try the next house," I said.

The man at the next house knew Tomas as well, and obligingly went to check his drawers. He returned holding some bright red-and-green boxer shorts with a set of tongs.

"I didn't want to touch them," he said. "Are they poisonous?"

"Underwear, or Fuzzles?" I asked.

"You're funny," he said, but he said "funny" as if it meant "strange." He dropped the boxer shorts inside the pot. "I don't need those back."

The next house was the same story, only this time it was an orange pair of underwear, and there were three smaller Fuzzles inside them. When the lady showed it to us, three pairs of eyes peered out of the leg holes.

"I think they're nesting," she said. "Do they normally live in hammocks or something like that?"

"Nobody knows what they normally live in," I replied. "But that's a good idea."

The house after that didn't have any Fuzzles in it, nor

the one after, but at the one after *that* we struck Fuzzle gold. When the woman went to check her underwear drawer, we heard a mighty scream. It was so piercing that both Tomas and I went running inside to see if something terrible had happened. The woman stood in a very fancy bedroom, staring in horror at the top drawer of her dresser. Flames roared out of it.

"Tongs!" I ordered. "Then drop the Fuzzles in the pot!"

The woman ran out of the room and returned with a large pair of barbecue tongs. She fished out a pair of fancy purple underwear. Fire shot out of both leg holes like a dual flamethrower. Tomas lifted the pot lid, and she dropped the underwear in. Then she retrieved another flaming pair. And another. The pot was filling up, and the dresser was still producing Fuzzles. Plus, some of them kept on burning even after they were dropped inside the pot.

"Ow!" Tomas said. "The handle's getting hot! There are too many to tickle!"

Plus, the dresser was still on fire. The smoke detector overhead began to shriek. Any Fuzzle that wasn't already ignited went up in flames.

Far too many to tickle.

The woman clapped her hands to her cheeks. "Oh, dear! I think I need to call 911! I must find my purse!"

"Where's the bathroom?" I shouted. "I'll pour some water on this!"

She pointed. As she ran to find her purse—and her phone, I guess, inside it—I ran into the equally fancy bathroom. There was nothing to put water in except for her toothpaste holder, so I began to make trips back and forth. Soon her underwear drawer was entirely doused, but the drawers below still seemed to be smoldering.

Outside, a fire engine wailed. Unexpectedly, the fancy lamp on top of the lady's fancy dresser caught on fire too, and the lightbulb exploded with a brittle bang. Somewhere, the lady began to shriek again, a fancy sort of shriek. It felt like every sound that could possibly happen was happening. Tomas seemed to agree with the Fuzzles, because he did the Tomas version of bursting into flame. He kneeled beside the smoking saucepan and covered his ears.

A fireman charged into the room. "How many of you are there?"

Tomas didn't reply because his ears were covered, and I didn't reply at first because I was just staring. Then I replied, "Two! And a lady. And a lot of Fuzzles."

"You need to get out!" he said.

"We were just trying to help!"

He said, "This is way too much for two kids. This is too much for any of us, probably. It's a disaster."

CHAPTER
6

Magical Ducks Are Terrible People

Luckily for everyone's underwear, Aunt Emma came up with a plan that evening. We were going to pack up all the Fuzzles and take them to a little island in the middle of Two Duck Lake. It wasn't a perfect plan—the Fuzzles couldn't stay there forever—but it was at least a place to put them while Cloverton came up with a better plan. And the island, even though it was small, could still hold more Fuzzles than the clinic.

"Would you like to help?" Aunt Emma asked me.

She didn't really have to ask.

An hour later, she and Callie drove off in the clinic van to collect a few more Fuzzles from the neighbors, and Tomas and I set off on our way to Two Duck Lake with Mr. Randall, one of Aunt Emma's friends. Mr. Randall's pickup truck was very large and very metal. Fuzzle-proof.

Off we went. Mr. Randall played some country music. I drew a Fuzzle on the back of my hand. Tomas scratched a rash on his arm. And the Fuzzles bounced along calmly in metal animal crates in the back of the truck.

Things seemed to be going well. Things were going well enough, in fact, that I was able to think about how we might spend the evening if we didn't have to return to a clinic full of Fuzzles. Callie had said something about a taco night when I first arrived, and I loved tacos. Plus I was starting to make friends with Regent Maximus. Maybe I could read him some entries from the *Guide*, so he'd know he didn't have to be afraid of things like Peruvian Squash Bunnies or Lightning-Hooved Deer. I even had time to feel a tiny bit homesick, even though I didn't exactly understand why. I was used to my parents going on long trips, and I was very interested in the magical-animal events here at Cloverton. I wouldn't have expected to feel a pang in my chest when I thought about home. Maybe I would ask Aunt Emma if she thought tonight would be a good night to try to check in with my parents.

As we approached the bigger highway, we hit a bump in the road, which brought my thoughts back to the present. The smell of warm fur wafted into the cab. I peered in the passenger-side mirror. No smoke. So far, so good? Maybe?

But as the truck got to full speed on the highway, the Fuzzles suddenly began to scale the crate walls.

Sudden movement was never a good sign.

"Uh-oh," Tomas said.

"What's happening back there?" Mr. Randall asked.

Neither Tomas nor I answered, because we weren't sure. The Fuzzles clung to the tops of the crates. They began to hum. Their fur flapped wildly in the wind. Every time the truck hit a bump, their humming hit a bump too.

Hhhhhhhhhmmmmm-heck!-hhhhhhhmmmmmm.

"They like it!" I exclaimed.

They really did! The Fuzzles were humming with *excitement*.

But then one of them began to smoke.

And then another one.

Soon clouds of smoke roiled from the back of the humming pickup truck. A single Fuzzle burst into flame.

"Oh, *no*," Tomas wailed.

The flaming Fuzzle was still humming happily. Other Fuzzles followed its lead, bursting into flame like corn kernels exploding into popcorn. Soon there was so much fire in the truck bed that it was hard to look directly at the Fuzzles. Tomas aimed his fire extinguisher out the back window and sprayed, but it didn't seem to do much—all the powder got blown away too fast. It scudded off the back of the pickup truck, like we were a disintegrating parade float.

A disintegrating parade float that was on fire.

On my hand, I jotted a hasty note to myself to remember to add this to my Fuzzle page in the *Guide*. It wasn't just fear that made Fuzzles catch fire—excitement could do it too.

Another car pulled alongside us. The lady in the passenger seat rolled down her window and called kindly, "Did you know that you have a truck full of animals on fire?"

"I did, but thanks," Mr. Randall called back.

"Slow down!" I told him. "The wind is making it worse!"

"I've seen worse than a truck bed of flaming lint rabbits!"

"Please slow down!" Tomas and I said at once.

"Okay, okay," Mr. Randall said. He slowed down.

Sure enough, as the wind stopped playing with the Fuzzles' fur, they grew less excited. The fires slowly died down until only a few of the Fuzzles were glowing like embers.

Tomas scratched his rash in a relieved sort of way, and I let out a big breath.

By the time Mr. Randall had offloaded us at our final destination, there was not a smoldering Fuzzle among them. We had made it to Two Duck Lake.

Everyone's been to a place like Two Duck Lake. It's one of those public lakes that people like to visit—locals, not tourists. There's a gravel parking area with a faded wooden map of hiking trails, rickety boat docks, and faded picnic benches. Mostly it's the kind of place where some people come to jump in the water and go "Wahoo!" and other people say, "Ew, don't splash that brown water on me."

Our final destination was the island right in the lake's center. It was tiny, but so were Fuzzles, so it would work nicely. Mr. Randall paddled us and the Fuzzles across the lake in a little metal canoe, then gave me his phone so I could call Aunt Emma and tell her we'd arrived.

"This is my first real job," Tomas remarked as I finished the call and shoved the phone into my pocket. He was helping unload the crates and had a small wad of tissue stuffed into each nostril. He'd told me this would keep him from inhaling the deadly dander of the Georgia Swamp Cretin, which he'd heard had been seen near the lake.

"I like—*oof*—that they—*oof*—trust us with something so—*oof*—important," I said, jumping in to help. All of the fire had welded the metal crates shut, so both Tomas and I had to yank on the closest crate door to get it open. As soon as we did, a batch of Fuzzles rolled out happily, leaving furry drag marks in the sand. Immediately, two squirrels (possibly Fancy Winged Squirrels, but I couldn't see their backs to tell) began to chatter in the trees overhead.

I heard one of them mutter, "Well, there goes the neighborhood."

They probably weren't wrong. I felt a little bad about taking over their little island. But squirrels could live anywhere, especially Fancy Winged Squirrels. Fuzzles couldn't seem to live anywhere without causing problems.

As Mr. Randall inspected the shoreline to make sure there was nothing really important the Fuzzles could destroy, Tomas and I sat on the sand and watched the Fuzzles roll around and bask in the sun.

"What now?" Tomas said. "This island can hold a lot of Fuzzles, but it can't hold *infinity* Fuzzles."

He had a point. I kicked at the dirt as a flock of ducks floated close to shore. Emerald Dunking Ducks. They have super-shiny head feathers made out of actual emeralds and are pretty common in public ponds. Even though they were pretty, I wasn't happy to see them. They're terrible.

Terribly judgmental, that is.

They don't actually have mustaches. I just drew those in because I really don't like them. Trust me, you'll understand why in a second.

Emerald Dunking Duck

Head is covered in real
emeralds, adding up to
2 pounds to body weight

Giant furry mustaches

Quacking has distinct,
muttering sound

Ducks use their powerful
feet for fighting; flock
disputes are settled by dunking
one another—whichever duck is
dunked farthest "loses" and moves
down in flock hierarchy

Particular tastes in bread; many prefer
multigrain and rye

SIZE: 20" at top of head
WEIGHT: Males 6 lbs, females 5 lbs.
DESCRIPTION: The Emerald Dunking Duck
is a species of wild duck commonly
found in the southern United States.
In the 1950s, ladies considered it
fashionable to keep these in their
gardens. Unfortunately, this particular
species does not tame well, and
hospitals report Duck attack injuries
increased tenfold until they were
banned from homes in 1963.

As this flock paddled up, all of the shiny green heads turned toward shore and muttered among themselves. To Tomas, they must have sounded like ordinary ducks quacking back and forth. But this was what I heard:

"Can you believe that girl's dress? Does she really think yellow is her color?"

"She looks like a mallard duckling. Speaking of mallards, did you see that family of mallards by the docks? I am pretty sure they have lake fleas because they look so shabby."

"Oh! Shabby! That reminds me of that grandmother we saw. Did you see her toenail polish? Is that what she considers fashion?"

"The times are changing."

"Changing."

"For the worse."

"Except for us."

"Yes."

"Oh, look at that boy with tissues in his nose and that weird girl staring at us."

"Maybe they have bread."

"I don't think they have bread. They look too stupid to have remembered to bring food to the island."

"That girl wouldn't share bread with us, anyway. I can tell. She's staring at us like we're pests. She's the pest. Humans and lake fleas! They're all so—"

I couldn't take it anymore. I said, "Hey! I can hear you, you know!"

Tomas blinked. "I didn't say anything."

"Not you! The *Ducks*."

The line of floating Ducks blinked at me. One of them said, "You can understand us?"

"Yes," I replied, as Tomas watched.

"Everything we said?" one of the other Ducks asked.

"Yes."

The Ducks looked at one another. Then the first one said, "So don't you agree that that girl in the blue bathing suit looks like a potato?"

I jumped up. "No! That's a horrible thing to say about someone. Why are you always so horrible?"

The Ducks muttered under their breath before drifting a little bit away and glancing back at me. I heard one of them say, "Well, I guess *someone's* feeling a little touchy today!"

There is absolutely nothing worse than a flock of judge-y magical Ducks.

"What did they say?" Tomas asked. He had one eyebrow raised. I couldn't tell if he believed me or not.

"I don't think you want to know," I replied. "They—"

Mr. Randall's phone—which was still in my pocket—rang. I looked at the screen: It was the clinic.

"Mr. Randall!" I shouted down the beach. He was depositing Fuzzles on the sand, one every few yards; they smoldered nicely without igniting anything. I held up the ringing phone for him to see. "It's the clinic!"

"Go ahead and answer. Might be your aunt calling back," Mr. Randall said, then went back to dropping Fuzzles.

I tapped the "answer" button. "Mr. Randall's phone, Pip speaking."

"Pip? It's me." I recognized Callie's voice at once. She said, "You and Tomas and Mr. Randall need to come back quick."

"Why?"

"Because Mrs. Dreadbatch is here—sorry, ma'am—Mrs. Dreadbotch—is here and she's mad. Something about a flaming truck?" Callie's voice was irritated, and I could hear Mrs. Dreadbatch talking—well, yelling—in the background. Now that I thought about it, her voice was an awful lot like those Ducks.

"Pip? Are you there?" Callie asked. "On the phone, you have to *talk*."

"I'm here. We just dropped the Fuzzles off. Mr. Randall's almost done."

"Seriously, Pip." Now Callie whispered right into the phone. "She's super-mad. She says since she's high up in

S.M.A.C.K.E.D., she's allowed to personally arrest Mom and Mr. Randall. Something about 'reckless transportation of flammable material.' Hurry."

" 'Flammable material'! They're *animals*!"

"Something wrong, Pip?" Mr. Randall asked, rejoining us. He set down an empty Fuzzle crate and dusted off his hands. "That's quite a serious face you've got on there."

"Mrs. Dreadbatch is at the clinic, and she's mad."

"I know Mrs. Dreadbatch," Mr. Randall said. He looked more grave than he had when driving a truck full of flaming Fuzzles. He said, "We better get back there."

There were a few people in the waiting room when we got back—a lady with a Multicolored Mongoose, a man with a very talkative Phoenix on his arm, and a pregnant lady quietly reading one of the brochures.

Then I spotted Mrs. Dreadbatch standing at the counter. Her back was to me as she spoke to Callie. But when she turned, I saw *the face*. She was holding a handkerchief over her mouth and nose, and *still* I could see it. The *you're-in-trouble* face.

Dreadbatch pulled the handkerchief away from her mouth just long enough to spit, "I'd like to know, Joseph, why a rolling fire hazard just made its way through Cloverton?" She clapped the handkerchief back over her mouth. Everything about her posture indicated that something about the clinic was too gross to breathe in directly.

"What's this all about now?" Aunt Emma asked, pushing through the clinic's door, Bubbles right behind her. She had glittery gold goo all over her hands. When Dreadbatch saw it, she swayed a little and pressed the handkerchief so tightly to her face that her knuckles turned white. Personally, I thought the gold was way better than the purple HobGrackle sweat she'd seen on her last visit.

"I've had it, Emma!" Dreadbatch said. "We didn't have a single Unicorn in this town before you opened your clinic. Now you're transporting Fuzzles? In a truck? *On fire?*"

"They weren't on fire when we left the house," Tomas piped up—bravely, I thought. Dreadbatch glared at him so hard that he pulled out his inhaler and took a puff.

Aunt Emma scrubbed goo onto a towel. "Mrs. Dreadbatch, everyone in Cloverton brought their Fuzzles here. We can't house them, obviously. In fact, another fifty have come in since this morning. They'll be perfectly fine on the island in Two Duck Lake—they can't swim, and the island is big enough to hold hundreds and hundreds of them. What else were we supposed to do?"

Mrs. Dreadbatch shook her handkerchief in Aunt Emma's face. "You're *supposed* to destroy them!"

Destroy them? They didn't *mean* to burn everything down!

Aunt Emma looked rather thin-mouthed all of a sudden. "I am not an exterminator, Mrs. Dreadbatch. I'm a veterinarian."

Dreadbatch eyed the Phoenix with distaste before looking back to us. "Which is why S.M.A.C.K.E.D. will be hiring an exterminator from Marshview to deal with the problem. My organization is getting tired of paying visits to your clinic. So if you have any more of these *things*, please refrain from trotting them through town with no regard to your neighbors! A flaming truck! What if you'd run into someone's private property? Imagine the horror!"

"Are you questioning Mr. Randall's driving skills?" Aunt Emma asked. "He was a police officer for twenty years!"

"That's not the point, Emma! The *point* is that those creatures are unsafe. The *point* is that they need to be destroyed, not moved. The *point* is that—"

"I do not work for S.M.A.C.K.E.D., Mrs. Dreadbatch, so unless you have court papers that require me to handle the Fuzzles in a specific way, I'll continue to make do as I see fit. Unless you *do* have court papers?" Aunt Emma asked. She looked really angry now. "I didn't think so. I think you need to go now, Mrs. Dreadbatch."

"It's Dreadbotch!" Mrs. Dreadbatch snapped. "And please. As if I'd want to stay a minute longer than necessary in this place!" She waved an arm around the clinic as she stomped out, shoes clicking on the tile floor. "*Magical creatures*. If they're so magical, why do they need their own vet—" The door slammed, cutting her off.

"I hope that's the last we hear from *her*," Mr. Randall said.

But we all knew it wouldn't be.

CHAPTER
7

Like Science Class, With Fuzzles

The next day, I sat in the lobby with Callie, watching a new litter of Bitterflunks. They bounced around like rubber balls, sometimes bouncing right out of their playpen. They were rather difficult to contain.

Callie was eating a giant bag of candy for lunch; she had to keep knocking the Bitterflunks out of the way as they aimed for the blue candies. Her tongue was a million different colors.

I was eating a spoon of peanut butter while going over my Fuzzle notes. I'd added quite a lot to the bare Fuzzle page in the *Guide*, thanks to my observation and to Callie's information from the Internet. But I still didn't know why they were here. Or why they kept coming. A new metal trash can had already been filled with today's latest batch of Fuzzles. They liked being lumped up together, and now they hummed happily, harmonizing up and down the scale.

Bitterflunk

Large ears signify excellent hearing

Rubbery skin ensures the Bitterflunk bounces well, and reduces injury from impact

Bitterflunks curl body into ball while bouncing

Stubby tail doesn't get in the way of bouncing

Bitterflunks hold their feet with their front paws to ensure they remain tightly curled while bouncing

Always found in odd numbers. Often in packs involving the numbers 3 or 7, i.e., 31 or 17

SIZE: 2-3" without tail
WEIGHT: 2 oz.
DESCRIPTION: The Bitterflunk is one of the Americas' more delightful and fascinating species. These social animals travel by bouncing, sometimes up to 21 feet in the air. Their natural fearlessness and intense attraction to the color blue sometimes make them a pest in urban areas, but generally the Bitterflunk has adapted well to life alongside humans.

"Figure out how to get rid of those things yet?" Callie asked, swatting at a Bitterflunk. She missed, and it yelled "*Wheeeeee!*" as it rocketed to the ground. I caught the little creature as it bounced back up and tossed it back in the playpen. ("Wheeee!" it shouted again.) Callie appeared grudgingly respectful. "Nice one, Pip."

"Thanks," I replied, surprised. I handed the *Guide* to her so she could read what I'd added.

I didn't get it. Fuzzles didn't really eat—they just rolled over dust and digested it. Surely Cloverton dust wasn't any better than dust anywhere else. They didn't come here on a migration or to hibernate. And they were shy enough of people that it seemed like it would take a pretty good reason to make them move into a populated area.

Callie handed the *Guide* back to me. "I'm getting pretty sick of them."

"Hey! They don't *mean* to—"

"Oh, calm down. I don't want them to get exterminated either. I just want them to stop showing up in my underwear drawer. What if they lit up my collection of *Playbill*s?" She said that with wide eyes, like I would understand how serious it would be.

I didn't understand, but I nodded anyway. "I know they're dangerous. But it's horrible—they're just being Fuzzles! There has to be a way to convince them to leave."

eyes closed

Fuzzle

gets around
by rolling

eyes
disappear
completely
when
closed

doesn't
seem to
have
bones?

SIZE: 4-6"
WEIGHT: 1-4 oz

also
when
excited

DESCRIPTION: ~~Pest.~~
• catches fire when scared
• eats dust?
• sleeps 11 hours a day
• hums to communicate
(hums in key of E when excited,
      D minor when scared)
• travels in ~~herds~~ groups
• light brown or beige

- seems friendly

"Better figure it out fast. Mrs. Dreadbatch put flyers in everyone's mailbox that said the exterminators will be here at the end of the week."

That was barely any time at all!

I looked at the Bitterflunks, who were chasing one another in circles and shouting "Tag, you're it! Tag, you're it! Tag, you're it!" even though no one actually seemed to be it. The *Guide* said Bitterflunks were pests too—but they were also pets. Maybe if people started thinking of Fuzzles as pets, they wouldn't be so quick to want them exterminated. Maybe people would even start to *want* them around.

"Callie," I said. "I have an idea!"

Callie looked worried.

I explained to her my thoughts on Fuzzles as pets. She looked more worried.

"A pet? That might burn your house down?" she asked.

"All pets have drawbacks," I insisted. "Bitterflunks are always burrowing into walls, but people still keep *them* as pets. And tons of people have Fire-Breathing Manticores!"

"Tons of people think they can sing soprano too, but that doesn't make them right," Callie said. I put my hands on my hips, and she finally rolled her eyes. "All right, all right—let's say we want to convince people these things are pets. What's the hook? What makes people think 'YES—I want a pet Fuzzle!'?"

I plucked two Bitterflunks out of my hair ("Tag, you're it!" shouted both of them) and answered, "Let's make a list."

Callie insisted on being the list maker. I suspected it was because holding the clipboard made her feel very important. She used a different colored pen for each line.

Fuzzles are great pets because:
1) Cute
2) Don't smell (not counting the smoke)
3) Don't bite
4) Eat dust (cuts down vacuuming?)

Then we made a list of why they were bad pets—the things we needed to overcome. It was a short list.

Fuzzles are bad pets because:
1) Burst into flame (constantly)
2) Destroy your underwear

"Callie!" I said. "Those are sort of the same thing. You can't count the underwear as a whole second thing."

"Tell that to my underwear," Callie said, rolling her eyes. She tapped her pen on the edge of the clipboard. "So far, the *bad* list outweighs the *good* one. Maybe they can be trained? You know, to *not* catch on fire. Plenty of animals *can* bite, but they're trained not to."

"That's a great idea, Callie!" I said.

I must have laid on the enthusiasm a little too thick, because she replied, "You don't have to sound so surprised. I do know *something* about animals. All right, let's train one."

I'd never really trained an animal before, but I knew the basic idea. We had to reward them for behavior that we liked.

"What do Fuzzles like?" Callie asked. "We can't just throw dust at them."

"Tickling," I said. "We can tickle them when they do the right thing."

We chose a small Fuzzle from today's trash can load, figuring that if it were a baby, perhaps it would be easier to train. Then we sat down in the middle of the clinic lobby with the Fuzzle in a frying pan between us. It zipped up and down the sides like a skateboarder on a ramp—I guess it liked the slippery frying-pan surface.

I said, "Now we need something that might startle it.

Not something *too* loud at first. And then, when it doesn't catch fire, we'll tickle it."

"And if it *does* catch fire?" Callie asked. "Do we punish it?"

"No, no. Only—what do you call it? Positive reinforcement." I held up the lid to the pan. "We'll just wait for it to calm down. Now, what can we do that might startle—"

"I've got this." Callie cracked her knuckles and gave me a smug look. "I needed to practice my scales anyway. Ready?" Taking a big breath, she began to sing, *"Do-re-mi-fa-sol-la-ti-doooooooooo."*

In response, the Fuzzle rolled in circles around the frying pan. It didn't burst into flame, so I tickled it. As it hummed, I grinned up at Callie. "Great! Can you do it any louder?"

"Oh, please! *Do-re-mi-fa-sol-la-ti-dooooooooo!*"

"What is all this noise? I'm trying to nap!" a gruff voice snapped from behind the desk. Bubbles poked his head around the corner, saw Callie, and sighed heavily. Ruffling his feathers, he asked, "Do you suppose Fuzzles would make good earmuffs?"

"I think that's a little risky," I replied. Luckily, Callie didn't hear me, because she was singing again, a little louder this time. I tried to tickle the Fuzzle, but it didn't seem to be paying much attention to me. It rolled away from my fingers—

"*Do-re-mi*—"

The Fuzzle rolled in smaller and smaller circles. Faster and *faster* circles too.

Callie got louder.

Bubbles covered his ears with his wings.

"*Do-re-mi*—"

"Callie, wait, don't get any louder!" I said, but her eyes were shut and her hands thrown out dramatically. She took a deep breath—

"*Fa-sol-la-ti-DOOOOOOOOOO!*"

The Fuzzle shivered at the last note and then, *pow*, it burst into flames so fast that I couldn't even get the lid on the pan in time. Smoke curled up to the ceiling, Callie scrambled backward, and Bubbles laughed.

"Don't blame the Fuzzle," Bubbles said. "Callie's singing makes me want to explode too."

"Maybe they just take a while to train," I said hopefully, waving the smoke away with the pan lid as the Fuzzle calmed. "One session doesn't really count."

Callie coughed meaningfully. "Get real, Pip. No one's going to risk a fire every time they turn on the radio or slam a door, even if the Fuzzle can *eventually* be trained. Fire-Breathing Manticores almost never turn into flame-balls. Fuzzles *always* turn into flameballs."

I tried to think of a positive spin. "But . . . but . . . maybe that can be useful though! People need fire, don't they?"

Callie gave me a long look as she added two lines to the *bad* list—

Fuzzles are bad pets because:
1) Burst into flame (constantly)
2) Destroy your underwear
3) Can't be trained
4) Don't appreciate fine music

I thought that fourth thing was a matter of opinion, but I didn't say anything. I dragged my backpack closer. I scooped the Fuzzle out of the frying pan and into one of the backpack's outside pockets. It seemed enough like an underwear hammock that the Fuzzle should be happy.

"See? Maybe Fuzzles could be great for camping!" I suggested brightly. "You could backpack with them, like this, and then when you stop to make a camp, you can just startle them and *boom*! You've got a campfire!"

"Or *boom*, your backpack is on fire," Callie said.

"Well, you wouldn't just *say* 'boom' until you needed—"

"No—*your backpack is on fire*," Callie said, pointing. I rustled the backpack off and sure enough, the Fuzzle was smoldering a hole right through the outside pocket. When the hole had burned big enough, the Fuzzle rolled out onto the clinic floor, leaving a trail of melted linoleum behind it.

This was not going well.

By the time Aunt Emma emerged from the exam rooms for her lunch break, Callie had added a lot more to our lists.

Fuzzles are bad pets because:

1) Burst into flame (constantly)
2) Destroy your underwear
3) Can't be trained
4) Don't appreciate fine music
5) Like to be in groups, so you can't really have just one
6) If you look away for a minute, they hide in some small place
6a) Like your underwear drawer
7) The smoke smells really bad after a while
8) The batteries in your smoke detector will be dead by the end of the day

"What's this?" Aunt Emma asked, brushing past the front desk. Callie and I were using the Fuzzles' fire to roast marshmallows right in the middle of the lobby. Using Fuzzles to help roast marshmallows was the only thing we'd been able to add to the *good* list.

"Fuzzle training. Want a marshmallow?" I held up my marshmallow skewer to her—the one on the end was perfectly browned.

Aunt Emma accepted it. Through the marshmallow, she asked, "Any luck?"

Callie shook her head. "Nope. They just—hey!" she said when the Fuzzle went out. She waved her marshmallow skewer over it, then sang, *"Do-re-mi-fa-sol-la-ti-do!"*

The Fuzzle burst back into flame. Callie stuck the marshmallow into the fire, then waited till it was nearly burned to a crisp to pull it off and eat it.

"Well, *this* is a cool idea, at least!" Aunt Emma said.

With a snort, Callie handed her mother the *bad* list. Aunt Emma's eyes widened. I couldn't tell if she was impressed or worried about all the experimenting we'd done.

"I just thought if we could prove they were trainable, people would think of them as pets, not pests," I said.

"It happens sometimes, Pip," Aunt Emma said kindly. "People are always trying to make pets out of animals, and sometimes they're just happier in the wild."

"The wilds of my underwear drawer," Callie huffed.

"I suspect that if the Fuzzles could talk, they'd tell you their habitat was here long before your underwear drawer. Or this clinic! Or Cloverton!" Aunt Emma pointed out. "I wish they *could* talk, actually—maybe they'd be able to talk some sense into Mrs. Dreadbatch!"

We all sighed. None of us believed anyone could talk sense into Mrs. Dreadbatch.

CHAPTER
8

A Total Lack of Dragons

The Fuzzle situation wasn't improving, and everyone was getting sick of roasted marshmallows. Even me, and that's really saying something.

I couldn't believe how many Fuzzles we'd found, and still, every day more poured into the clinic in trash cans and buckets and old toaster ovens. Mr. Randall took a load to Two Duck Island in the afternoons, which meant Mrs. Dreadbatch came to yell about things in the evenings, which meant we were all tired and pretty Fuzzled-out by the time the sun went down.

"I can't do it! I can't do it anymore!" Callie said one morning. Her voice was already hectic. "I dreamed about them last night, Pip. I dreamed I was onstage, only instead of people in the audience, it was Fuzzles. *A theater full of Fuzzles!*"

Callie was starting to crack. I tried to look understanding when the clinic door opened behind us.

"Add them to the pile in that bathtub!" Callie snapped without turning to look.

A voice replied, "Pile? Bathtub? I'm here about Regent Maximus. Just thought I'd pay him a visit."

"Mr. Henshaw!" I said, jumping to my feet.

He waved. Just as before, he wore a suit, and his hair was so perfectly combed it looked like plastic doll hair. His tie was the sort of bright blue that Bitterflunks couldn't resist. Immediately, every Bitterflunk in the playpen bounced off the walls and floor to land on it.

Mr. Henshaw looked as dignified as one could expect in this situation. "Pip, how's my Unicorn?"

"He's great," I said, with hardly any hesitation at all. I was getting better at talking to humans, especially when I got to talk about magical creatures. I went on, "Well, he's sort of great. He hides in the straw a lot. And when we had that little thunderstorm the other afternoon he thought he was going to drown. And he got his horn stuck in his feedbag on Tuesday. But other than that . . . Here, let me walk you to see him."

I glanced at Callie, who narrowed her eyes at Mr. Henshaw before saying to me, "While you're out there, Fuzzle the Griffins—I mean, feed the Griffins their Fuzzles—I mean, feed the Fuzzles—AH! JUST GIVE THE GRIFFINS SOME HAY!"

Mr. Henshaw looked scared. I hurried him out to the large animal stable.

Regent Maximus was in a stall between two Standard Griffins named Buzzer and Fleet.

"Oh, thank goodness you're here," Fleet called, so fast that it took me a moment to put together what she'd just said. She always talked fast. "He's been whimpering for an hour. At least an hour! He says there's a wasp in his stall."

"No, that was this morning," Buzzer said, poking his beak through the stall door. He looked grumpy. He always looked grumpy. "Now he says it was a Glowfly."

"They won't hurt you if you don't thrash about and bother them," I told Regent Maximus, who continued thrashing and bothering. I peered about in his stall for wasps or Glowflies but saw neither.

Mr. Henshaw looked bewildered. "Sorry, what?"

"No, no, no," I said swiftly. I tried to act natural, though I couldn't remember exactly how much I'd said out loud, or how long I'd been staring at the animals while they spoke to me. "Just, I was . . . letting the animals know I was here!"

Clipping a lead on to Regent Maximus's halter, I led him from the stall and into the backyard while Mr. Henshaw watched. Regent Maximus sidestepped a dandelion as if it were a cobra.

"My life!" Regent Maximus muttered in muted terror. "Oh, my life!"

Mr. Henshaw sighed. "I just don't think he's ever going to show. I had such hopes for him."

"Maybe with a little work," I said, patting Regent Maximus on the nose. He eyed a fly as it swept past us. His expression was deeply worried.

"You don't understand, Pip," Mr. Henshaw said. "I've hired trainers that cost more than most houses. *No one* has been able to calm him down. Unicorns are supposed to be majestic! They're supposed to be proud!"

"Sometimes *proud* isn't such a good thing when it comes to Unicorns," I said, thinking about Fortnight and Raindancer. "And anyway, maybe he just needs someone who can understand him," I said.

"And you understand him?"

I shrugged shyly. I *did* understand Regent Maximus better than most people. *That* I was definitely sure of.

Mr. Henshaw smiled. "How about this—see that board over there?" He pointed to a broken bit of fencing lying in the grass. "If you convince him to step over that board before he moves back in with me, I'll give you twenty dollars."

For some reason, this made me feel embarrassed. I quickly said, "Oh! I don't have to get *paid*! I'll do it for free."

He laughed. "That's not good business!"

"I'm not really a businessperson," I replied. "I'm more of a . . . researcher. I'd do it for the research."

"That's fair," Mr. Henshaw said. "Noble. Let's shake on it, then."

We shook hands just as Aunt Emma walked outside.

"Please tell me you didn't just sell my niece that Unicorn," she said, pointing at our clasped hands. "I can't feed any more large animals."

Mr. Henshaw's eyes sparkled. "Not yet—but that's an excellent backup plan, if his show career doesn't work out. I'll give her a good deal."

"Don't tempt her! Pip is as animal crazy as I am," Aunt Emma said, which made me feel both shy and pleased. Before I could decide which feeling was stronger, she changed the conversation to talk about stable construction and square footage and building permits.

I stopped listening and turned to Regent Maximus. In a low voice, I said, "All right, Regent Maximus. I'll give you a chunk of honeycomb the size of my hand if you go over that board."

"I will die," Regent Maximus said. "Splinter. Nail. Abscess. Tetanus. That garbage truck."

The truck was six houses away. There was no possible way it could kill him. I tried to explain this to Regent

Maximus, but it turned out that *talking* to a Unicorn was a very different thing from *convincing* a Unicorn. I couldn't help but think about what a bad job of convincing I'd done during the Unicorn Incident.

The grown-ups were still talking. Mr. Henshaw, in a quite different voice from before, suddenly said, "Emma, I was thinking—would you like to go to dinner sometime? There's this fabulous new Italian—"

"Oh, Bill, I'm flattered," Aunt Emma said, her cheeks turning red. "Really, I am. But I'm still married to Grady." She held up her left hand and flashed her wedding ring.

"I understand," Mr. Henshaw said, but as if he did not understand. "Remember that it's been seven years . . ."

"I know," Aunt Emma said. "Believe me, I know."

It was strange to hear someone talk about Uncle Grady. Most of the time we didn't talk about my uncle.

And because we didn't talk about my uncle, we also didn't talk about dragons.

There are no dragons in *Jeffrey Higgleston's Guide to Magical Creatures* . . . because they don't exist. I mean, I'd love it if they did—there are all sorts of old stories about them, and every once in a while, a crazy story appears in the paper about how some old lady out in the desert spotted one. But the truth is that no one reputable has seen one in living memory, and no one ever finds skeletons. And most importantly, no one ever finds dragon poop.

Everything poops.

So there are no dragons. And yet, seven years ago, Aunt Emma's husband, my uncle Grady, set off into the deserts of Texas and Mexico, looking for them. For a long time, he kept in touch—he called, or sometimes wrote Aunt Emma romantic letters. But then one day, the calls and letters stopped. Really *stopped*, just like that.

Was he dead? Was he alive? Did he need help? Did he ever find any dragon poop?

These questions had gone unanswered for seven years.

"Thanks for the, uh, invitation though," Aunt Emma said, trying so hard to make her voice sound casual and airy that it sounded the opposite. "Give me a call when the stable is all ready for Regent Maximus!"

I saw Callie standing suspiciously in the doorway to the clinic. Her eyes were laser-death on Mr. Henshaw.

Mr. Henshaw smiled warmly despite this. "And, Pip! Don't get too discouraged with Regent Maximus. I appreciate that you're even trying."

In the background, Regent Maximus suddenly shouted in terror. It sounded like a frightened whinny to everyone else, but I, of course, could understand him perfectly as he screamed, "Why! Why is the sky so *blue* today? What does it *mean*?"

I said, with considerably more confidence than I felt, "Just you wait. He'll be a new Unicorn the next time you see him."

Miniature Silky Griffins Are Also Terrible People

"It's. A. Piece. Of. Wood. Literally. It's a piece of wood. You're surrounded by them all day, every day, when you're in the stable," I said, dropping my forehead into my hand.

I was trying to be patient with Regent Maximus, but we'd been out here since lunchtime. It was hot and sticky, and gnats kept flying into my eyes. My entire arm was already covered with Fuzzle doodles I'd done while waiting out Regent Maximus's many meltdowns. This board business hadn't seemed like such an impossible task when I'd made the deal, but apparently Mr. Henshaw knew his Unicorn better than I'd thought.

Tomas, who was standing over on the clinic's back step to avoid allergy bubbles, pointed out, "In fact, the wood used to build the stable is bigger. This is just a little piece of wood."

"Bigger pieces?" Regent Maximus said, flicking a

fearful ear toward the stable. His eyes widened. He started to tremble.

Great. Now he was afraid of the stable too.

Regent Maximus wasn't the only thing on my mind. I was starting to feel a little more nervous about the Fuzzle situation. A lot more nervous, actually. We were one day closer to the exterminators' arrival and we were no closer to a Fuzzle solution. We hadn't seen Mrs. Dreadbatch again, but Aunt Emma had showed me a Cloverton newspaper article over breakfast. The tiny Cloverton museum had caught fire the night before, and all of the historical Civil War uniforms had been destroyed—I guessed Fuzzles would settle for wool uniforms when they couldn't find any underwear. S.M.A.C.K.E.D. had called for a community meeting over the Fuzzle situation. Apparently they needed a majority vote in order for the extermination to go forward.

Extermination! Even the word sounded terrible.

Aunt Emma had said she'd go to the community meeting and talk about how well the habitat on the island was working for the moment. But she'd looked worried. She knew it wasn't a permanent solution.

"No," Regent Maximus was saying to Tomas. "No-no-no-no-no."

"Why is he making noises at me?" Tomas asked. "I didn't say anything!"

"His face!" the Unicorn said. "That boy was about to ask me to get closer and I won't! I—no-no-no!"

I grimaced at him. It was hard to believe that he was the same species as the Barreras' Unicorns. Regent Maximus slouched as much as a four-legged animal could slouch, and his rainbow forelock dribbled uncertainly over one eye. Also, Tomas had put one of his brothers' white tube socks over the Unicorn's horn, which made him look even less noble. Tomas told me the sock was to make training Regent Maximus safer. I didn't think a tube sock would stop what Jeffrey Higgleston had called "the purest weapon in the natural world," but Tomas was insistent.

Tomas switched to our previous topic of conversation: Fuzzles. "Maybe the you-know-whats are flying—well, rolling—south for the season? Like how birds do?" Earlier, we discovered the word *Fuzzle* sent Regent Maximus into a blind panic. Literally blind. He'd squeezed his eyes shut, then started running. Luckily, he hit the hay bale rather than the tractor right beside it.

"Nobody has mentioned anything online about a migration. And *somebody* would've noticed if they did it every year," I replied. "Things don't just suddenly decide to migrate."

Tomas pulled a little motorized fan out of his pocket and waved it back and forth in front of his face. He looked at me. "What? Heatstroke can send you into cardiac arrest in minutes."

I wished Tomas could have a conversation with Regent Maximus. I thought they'd have a lot to talk about.

The clinic's back door cracked open. Bubbles trudged through, looking indignant, and Callie's voice followed him: "Go on! If I find out who gave you pineapple, they're dead. Now the whole office smells—" The door slammed shut.

Bubbles rolled his eyes, then laid down on the back step right beside Tomas. Under his breath, the Miniature Griffin muttered, "Smells better than her nail polish." Then a small noise erupted from his rear end.

Tomas frowned. Regent Maximus shuddered.

Bubbles asked me, "What's going on out here?"

I said, "We're trying to teach Regent Maximus to go over that board over there."

Bubbles chewed on a claw with his beak as he studied the board. "You mean, jump over it?"

"No. Walk over it."

"And he . . . can't?"

"He's nervous," I explained politely, since now Regent Maximus was listening. "About splinters. And tripping. And there were some ants near it earlier—"

"*Unicorns,*" Bubbles interrupted, looking thoroughly disgusted. He closed his eyes, though I could tell he was not sleeping.

I turned back to Regent Maximus. "Think about it, Regent Maximus. Mr. Randall's going to be here soon, and we'll have to leave to take today's Fuzzles to Two Duck Lake. This could be your last chance to go over the board today!"

Regent Maximus's nostrils flared. "Why? What's going to happen later today? Earthquake? Killer bees? Shipwreck? *What do you know?*"

"All right," Bubbles broke in grouchily. "Let's do this." Rising, he stretched, extending his claws and bristling his feathers. "Hey, Unicorn! What's his name? Regent Maximus? Regent—that's a long name. How about instead of Regent What-evers-mus, I call you . . ." He hunched forward, ready to pounce, and said, "Dinner."

"What?" I asked, confused.

"Dinner," Regent Maximus echoed, with a note of hysteria in his voice. "*Dinner.*" He eyeballed Bubbles, trying to decide if this twenty-pound creature was really a threat.

Flexing his small claws, Bubbles twitched his tail from side to side.

"Pip! Pip, hide me!" Regent Maximus screamed, prancing behind me. He stuck his head under my arm to keep an eye on Bubbles. I felt him quivering. His tube-socked horn was right in front of me. It was quivering too.

"I haven't had a good Unicorn in ages," Bubbles said, low and menacing. "I can't wait. Do we have any steak sauce, Pip?"

"Bubbles," I said. "I don't think—"

Regent Maximus was no longer forming coherent sentences—he was just shouting words: "Pip! Dinner! Eat! Hide! *STEAK SAUCE!*"

Bubbles sprang forward—sort of. He was too old to actually *spring*, so he just heaved himself off the back stoop.

It was enough.

Regent Maximus reared, rainbow mane waving like a flag behind him. He took off like a shot. Right at the board in the grass.

He leaped over it like it was nothing.

Tomas let out a loud "Whoop!" and jumped to his feet. Regent Maximus didn't even notice what he'd just done—he continued on, wailing "Steak sauce!" at the top his lungs. When he reached the fence on the edge of the property, he shot a furtive look back at Bubbles, then dove behind a trough.

"You're welcome," Bubbles said to me. He pulled himself back onto the stoop with a yawn. "Unicorns. I'd rather have HobGrackles."

"Don't look so smug," I shot back, even crankier than before. "That Unicorn didn't *learn* anything."

Tomas joined me, and together we walked over to retrieve Regent Maximus. He was still wedged behind the trough, which would have been a pretty good hiding spot, if it weren't for the clearly visible tube sock sticking up above it.

"Why did Bubbles attack?" Tomas asked, because of course he hadn't understood a word of Bubbles's plan.

I explained it as Tomas removed a handful of fruit-flavored cough drops from his pocket, then placed a tantalizing trail of them from Regent Maximus's hiding spot out into the yard. I heard the Unicorn make snuffling smelling noises behind the trough, but I guess he wasn't tempted enough to come out just yet.

Tomas shrugged and stuck the last cough drop in his mouth. He said, "Well, you have to admit, the idea of getting eaten is pretty scary. I'd probably run too if something said it wanted to eat me with steak sauce. Especially since I'm allergic to steak sau—"

My bad mood suddenly melted away, replaced by excitement. "Tomas! That's it!"

"My steak sauce allergy? It's really an allergy to the caramel coloring—"

"No! The Fuzzles!" I clapped my hands together. "I think I know why they're here!"

Escape and Other Bright Ideas

The Fuzzles were afraid.

Not of *everything*, like Regent Maximus was, but rather, they were afraid of being eaten. I was sure they had *fled* to Cloverton . . . from a predator. Trouble was, I didn't have the tiniest clue what ate Fuzzles.

Still, it was a start. I decided the next step was to talk it out with Aunt Emma, and I got my opportunity that evening.

After the clinic was closed, Aunt Emma took me and Callie out to Two Duck Lake. She needed to check on the Fuzzles, so we decided to have a picnic dinner on the island too. She wasn't the best at cooking though, so dinner was foil-wrapped baked potatoes with everything from the refrigerator drawers chopped up and put on them.

As we landed on the shore—thankfully, the Emerald Dunking Ducks seemed to have bedded down elsewhere, taking their judge-y comments with them—the Fuzzles crowded close, just out of reach. It was hard to tell what they were thinking, but they seemed curious. Aunt Emma lifted a few up, holding her stethoscope to each one, then shining a mini-flashlight in their eyes.

"They're doing so well here!" she said. "It's too bad we'll run out of room soon."

She didn't say *Too bad they'll be exterminated soon.* But I could tell she was thinking it.

Callie flopped down on the shore and opened her potato, then sighed. "Great. This thing's cold as a dead polar bear." Annoyed, she wrapped her potato back up and tossed it onto a pile of nearby Fuzzles, who lit up instantly.

"*Callie!*" admonished Aunt Emma.

Callie blinked. "What? If they can roast marshmallows, they can heat potatoes."

There seemed to be an important difference between roasting a marshmallow *over* a Fuzzle and chucking a potato on its head, but the Fuzzles didn't seem to mind. Still, Aunt Emma and I placed our foil packages more carefully among the Fuzzles instead of tossing them like Callie. When the potatoes had warmed and we were tucking into our food, I asked, "Aunt Emma, do Fuzzles have any natural predators?"

She picked a piece of apple off her potato and chewed

it thoughtfully. "Well, lots of creatures find them delicious, actually. That's why Fuzzles catch fire. They need some dramatic defense mechanisms to protect them since they aren't very fast and don't have teeth or claws to fend off large predators."

"What sort of large predators?"

She thought about it. "Wild Morks, I suppose. They have special lining in their mouths to allow them to eat animals with spines, and it works to keep the flames from burning them so badly. And plain old crocodiles will eat them if they can get ahold of them, because they pull them underwater. Grims, if Fuzzles are in the path of the pack's migration. Sometimes Wild Hobs . . ."

As Aunt Emma went on musing about Wild Hobs for a moment (and Callie went on sighing heavily about all the magical-creatures talk happening), I heard what sounded like a splash close by.

"Did you hear that?" I asked.

Aunt Emma and Callie didn't bother saying "What?" They both shut up in a hurry and listened. Sure enough, another splash sounded above the hushed buzzing of dusk insects.

"Glassfish?" Aunt Emma suggested. "There aren't many mosquitoes out, but maybe they're catching dragonflies."

There was another splash.

Glassfish

The carnivorous Glassfish consumes twice its weight in insects each day

Glassfish feed at the surface; when threatened by birds or other predators, they can rapidly transform into glass

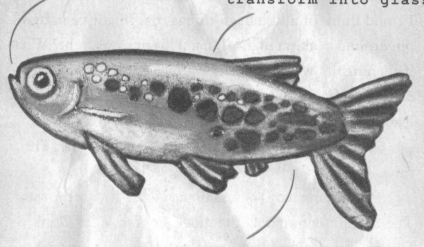

Glassfish are one of the longest-lived freshwater fish species; they do not appear to age when in their glass form

SIZE: 6"
WEIGHT: 1-2 oz.
DESCRIPTION: The Glassfish is a freshwater fish named for its ability to turn its skin to glass when under attack by predators. The Glassfish was widely fished in the late Middle Ages, when their glass bodies were made into noisy mobiles and used to drive away evil. The species has made a comeback, as the superstition died out in the

Aunt Emma whipped out two flashlights. I took one; Callie reached for the other, but Aunt Emma grabbed her hand instead. Together, the three of us forged to the shore, sweeping the flashlights back and forth. My heart was galloping too loudly to hear if there were any more splashes. I could think of all kinds of things that might be hanging out around a lake at night. What if Tomas was right? What if there really were Georgia Swamp Cretins around here? Sure, they weren't really deadly, but the bite of one could leave you limping for weeks!

(That wasn't in the *Guide*. Tomas had told me. Three times.)

Aunt Emma cast her flashlight to and fro on the sand. The beam illuminated the flock of Emerald Dunking Ducks. They bobbed in the shallows, eyes shut, fast asleep, looking like a fleet of ships at harbor. One of them was muttering in his sleep: "... *so much better ... than those smaller ducks ... practically chickens ... barely even poultry ...*"

"I don't see anything," Aunt Emma whispered to me.

But I did. And I didn't need a flashlight to see it.

"There!" I hissed. Halfway between the shore of the island and the shore of the mainland, a tiny, impossible fire burned on top of the water.

It was a Fuzzle, of course. I pointed my flashlight at it. It swayed gently in the water, wiggling and twitching and scooting its butt (maybe . . . it was hard to tell which end of a Fuzzle was which) to force itself closer to shore.

"How is it doing that?" Aunt Emma asked. "Fuzzles don't swim!"

Callie's voice came from behind us, quite sour. "You'd better find out, because there go the rest of them."

We jerked to follow her gaze. Sure enough, a small fleet of Fuzzles sailed into the middle of the lake, half of them on fire.

My normally practical and unshakable aunt said, "Oh, *no*. How?"

I squinted at them and shined my flashlight at the closest one. It seemed even more magical than Fuzzles were supposed to be. Like they were hovering on top of the water.

But then, as another batch of Fuzzles floated by, my flashlight caught a glint of light. It didn't seem to be coming from the Fuzzle. It seemed to be coming from *under* the Fuzzle.

"It's the Glassfish!" I gasped. "They're riding on the Glassfish!"

Sure enough, when we trotted farther around the island, we saw that when the Glassfish came to the surface for insects, the Fuzzles leaped onto them. The Glassfish didn't seem to mind. Instead, they bobbed along like fire-proof little boats.

All of the Fuzzles seemed to know instinctively how to wiggle and shimmy and vibrate in just the right way to keep their Glassfish headed toward shore. As they grew closer to freedom, they began to hum, and as they began to hum, more and more of them caught fire.

"This is a disaster," Aunt Emma said. "If they get loose on shore, they could set the vacation cabins on fire. And we can't bring them back here, because obviously they can escape!"

Callie said, "This is just great. Nature! I love it! Just wait until Mrs. Dreadbatch hears about *this*."

Just the sound of her name made my blood run cold.

I asked, "Can you call Mr. Randall? Maybe he can bring down some fire extinguishers before anyone sees."

"Yes, yes," Aunt Emma said, sounding relieved. "That's a start. Can you try to scare away the rest of the Glassfish to keep any more from escaping while I try to get ahold of him?"

"How are we supposed to do *that*?" Callie demanded.

I pulled off my shoes and grimly began to roll up my pant legs.

"Oh, no way!" Callie said. "These are character shoes! For the stage! I was just breaking them in!"

Another batch of Fuzzles launched themselves onto more Glassfish swimming in the shallows. Without another word of protest, both Callie and I hurled ourselves after them, scattering the school just beneath the surface.

"Hello?" Aunt Emma said anxiously into the phone. "Joseph? We need your help! They're escaping—I know, I didn't think they were clever enough either—"

On the shore of the mainland, it seemed like help had already arrived. A pair of headlights suddenly blinded us. They were pointed right at the island. A silhouette climbed out. It was wearing heels. It was a bit melty looking.

Aunt Emma swung her flashlight up to illuminate the distant newcomer on the other shore.

Mrs. Dreadbatch.

"Ah *ha*!" Mrs. Dreadbatch cried, pointing furiously. "I *knew* it!"

And then the ground right in front of her caught fire.

It really was a small fire, all things considered—the first group of Fuzzles had finally rolled ashore. But that didn't stop Mrs. Dreadbatch from leaping back with a shriek-yell-curse. Whipping off her bright red blazer, she began beating the flames with it. All the noise and the waving shocked the other Fuzzles, causing them to light up, one after another, until they were like little campfires across the water.

"Come on!" Aunt Emma shouted, and Callie and I hurried into the canoe. Aunt Emma shoved us off before clambering in and paddling furiously. We'd barely struck the other shore when she jumped out, tripping a bit in the water as she rushed to help Mrs. Dreadbatch.

"They're everywhere! They're *everywhere*!" Mrs. Dreadbatch howled. Lights in the vacation cabins were flicking on and people were staring. And Mrs. Dreadbatch was right: The Fuzzles really *were* everywhere. Bushes rustled with them. The dirt paths seethed with them. They rolled around Mrs. Dreadbatch's feet; little flames licked at her ankles. Her panty hose had scorch marks on them, and there were big burned holes in her blazer.

"Mrs. Dreadbatch, you have to stop yelling! You're scaring them! You're making it worse!" Aunt Emma urged. Grabbing Mrs. Dreadbatch's arm, she tried to pull her away from the Fuzzle-filled shore. But Mrs. Dreadbatch's pointy high heels didn't work very well in the sand.

First her ankle twisted around. Then her leg. Then she whirled in a circle, overbalanced, and with a great flailing of arms tumbled to the ground. Her butt landed squarely on a flaming Fuzzle. Her pointy shoes flew off—I heard one splash into the lake—and she began to roll down the shore, backside lit with Fuzzle fire. With a yelp, Aunt Emma ran for her, but it was too late.

Mrs. Dreadbatch rolled straight into the lake.

Personally, I thought this was a good thing—the lake water, after all, put out the fire on her butt.

Mrs. Dreadbatch didn't see it that way.

She reared up from the water, grabbing the side of our canoe to hoist herself to a standing position. Gasping for air, she went all wide-eyed. Her mascara was running and there were pond weeds stuck to her head.

Aunt Emma stood on the shore, still dripping, watching in shock. She wasn't the only one—all the vacationers had come out of their cabins and were staring.

Finally, Mrs. Dreadbatch said, "Ahhhhhhhhhh!" in a way that made me think she was going to charge Aunt Emma like an angry rhinoceros. Aunt Emma seemed to think so too, because she took a step back.

"That's it!" Mrs. Dreadbatch finally managed to form words. She slogged her way out of the lake, looking a bit like a Scottish Bog Wallow. I suspected she didn't eat slugs though, like the Wallows did. Well, she *probably* didn't, anyhow.

Callie and I kicked our legs over the side of the canoe and followed her onto the shore.

"You're not hurt, Mrs. Dreadbatch. It's all right!" Aunt Emma said hopefully. Mr. Randall wheeled up with a truck full of fire extinguishers, but there was no point—

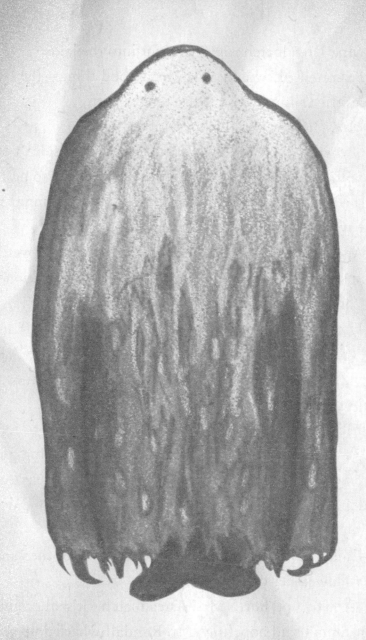

Scottish Bog
Wallow

now that Mrs. Dreadbatch wasn't beating them with a red blazer, the Fuzzles were happily rolling along the shore, fire-free.

"Not hurt? *Not hurt*? What, exactly, do you call *this*?" Mrs. Dreadbatch snapped, pointing to the scorch mark on her butt. It'd burned straight through to her flowery underwear. "Tomorrow. The exterminators are coming *tomorrow*. S.M.A.C.K.E.D. will pay them whatever they want. These Fuzzles are *dangerous*, and they clearly can't be contained. What if they'd burned down one of the cabins? Or my house? Or your precious *clinic*? *Then what?*"

I thought Aunt Emma would have some sort of quick response, so I was confused when Mrs. Dreadbatch made it all the way to her Cadillac and I still hadn't heard my aunt say anything.

I turned to her.

Aunt Emma looked defeated and soggy. She tucked her hair behind her ear and nodded quietly. Mr. Randall patted her shoulder comfortingly. Then they both started toward the car.

"Wait!" I called after them. "Aunt Emma! You can't just give up!"

Aunt Emma sighed. "Pip, as much as I hate to agree with Mrs. Dreadbatch—and I *really* hate to agree with her—she's right. It isn't safe. Someone could get seriously hurt. It isn't fair to the Fuzzles, I know, but it has to be this way."

I didn't know what to say. Callie, Mr. Randall, and Aunt Emma began gathering up armfuls of Fuzzles and putting them in the back of Mr. Randall's truck. It would take far more than one truckload to hold them now.

"Where are we headed with them?" Mr. Randall asked.

Aunt Emma still sounded depressed. "Back to the clinic, for now. We can watch them there. And we can keep them comfortable until the exterminators arrive to . . ."

She didn't say the rest. She didn't have to.

I refused to help put the Fuzzles in the truck. I wouldn't be any more a part of this than I already was. Stomping back down to the lake, I sat on the shore with my chin on my knees. The lake water lapped at my toes, and my throat felt all lumpy from trying to hold back tears. Then, to make things worse, the newly woken flock of Emerald Dunking Ducks floated nearby, muttering to one another.

"Did you see that lady fall into the water? I wonder if I can find her shoe. Those were nice shoes."

"Oh, yes, very nice. I liked her necklace too. Looked like emerald."

"Indeed!"

"Maybe with those Fuzzles gone, we'll get back to some peace and quiet around here."

"Well, if we can get the loud kids to leave too. They splash too much. Upsets the silt."

"No one shows any regard for the silt. Remember that black dog? He tromped right into it! Who does he expect to clean all that up?"

"You know what I bet he has?"

"Lake fleas," both Ducks said at once.

I glowered at them. I must have looked pretty serious, because they gave me a pointed look, then floated away, snickering to each other about my hair.

"Don't you dare say I have lake fleas!" I yelled after them. Lake fleas. I wasn't even sure they existed. Those Ducks just wanted something to complain about. I bet that dog didn't even bother the silt—

My head snapped up.

Dog. A black dog.

I looked down at the nearest Fuzzle—it was right next to my leg. "Hey, Fuzzle? Can you tell me why you are all in Cloverton suddenly?"

Of course, I had tried to talk to them before, back at the clinic, and they'd only hummed at me. I figured they just couldn't talk or wouldn't talk. I guess I figured that something so small just didn't understand things.

The same way lots of people figure some*one* so small, like me, just doesn't understand things.

"I know you probably tried to tell me before," I said. "Or, er, one of you. But I'm listening now, I promise. Why are you here?"

The Fuzzle rolled closer to me. Another joined it, and another, and another. And they hummed together, but this time I knew it wasn't really humming. They were *speaking*.

"*Grrrrrrrr-immmmmmmmmmm,*" they harmonized.

And now I knew exactly what they'd been trying to tell me, because I knew exactly what a Grim was, thanks to *Jeffrey Higgleston's Guide to Magical Creatures*.

It was, as I thought all along, a predator. A predator that looked an awful lot like a big black dog.

A very frightening, very enormous, very toothy, big, black, *magical* dog.

CHAPTER 11

Things Get Grim

I told Aunt Emma as soon as we had gotten the Fuzzles settled down back at the clinic, but she didn't believe me.

"Pip, didn't you read the rest of the section in the *Guide*? Grims have set migration patterns. They spend the winters in Mexico, and they go to a colony in the mountains of North Carolina every summer. They're famous for their migration. They don't wander."

"But what about the rogue Grim?" I asked. "Couldn't it be a rogue Grim? No wonder they wanted to escape the island, if there's a rogue Grim wandering around Two Duck Lake!"

Aunt Emma said, "It's not impossible, but it is not probable—and besides, we don't know they were escaping on purpose. One might have just rolled onto the Glassfish by accident, and the others followed. Fuzzles do tend to stick together like that. And anyway, it doesn't matter, Pip. It's too late now. It's too late to change anything."

Grim

Like the Ninja Dog, Grims are always pitch-black in color

Grims are double-coated: a soft layer of baby fur is closest to the skin and the external coat is made of coarse hairs stronger than metal

Grims will go through four sets of teeth in their lifetime, each set larger and harder than the last; an elderly Grim has teeth sharper than diamonds

Massive paws are much larger than those of domestic dogs

An adult Grim can leap over a 7-foot wall

Grims are very slow to mature—a juvenile Grim takes over seven years to reach full size and relies heavily on its packmates to protect and feed it

---

SIZE: 72" at shoulder
WEIGHT: 275-350 lbs.
DESCRIPTION: Grims are one of the most endangered—and dangerous—predators. These stealthy, slinky animals are the result of a long-ago crossing between a Dire Wolf and a Ninja Dog. Although social creatures, occasionally, a Grim will separate from his pack. These singled-out animals are called "rogue Grim." All Grims have been protected under the Endangered Magical Species

"But we have all night! We could go looking for a Grim!" I insisted.

"Pip," she said, putting her hand on my shoulder—this is what grown-ups do sometimes when they are trying to tell you something that you won't like—"I know this is a terrible situation. But we can't do any good traipsing around Cloverton at night looking for an animal that's not there. We *can* do some good by making sure the Fuzzles are not stressed out in the clinic and by going to the community meeting to make sure this never happens again."

She went into the clinic then, but it seemed to me like she was really only going there to be sad about the whole thing.

I went to my bedroom. But I didn't sleep. I lay in my bed and drew Fuzzles on my hands and tried to think of a plan. By the time the sun came up, I hadn't gotten much sleep, but I'd decided what I was going to do. If there was a Grim, I was going to find it and talk to it. I would convince it to leave Cloverton. And then the Fuzzles would return to the wild. Everyone—from the Fuzzles to Mrs. Dreadbatch's backside—would be safe.

There was only one catch. I needed transportation to find the Grim, and it was pretty obvious that Aunt Emma wasn't going to skip the community meeting to drive me around looking for it.

I had an idea.

But I wasn't sure if it was a good idea. My mother always said, "Think twice, act once." It hadn't worked very well with the whole Unicorn Incident thing. But this time I thought I'd think once and then have Tomas think once, and together we'd maybe make a not-stupid decision.

As soon as there was enough light to see by, I called Tomas. His mother answered and gave up the phone to him after a moment.

"Pip?" Tomas asked blearily. He sounded as if he had been woken up. Or perhaps like he was still asleep.

"You've got to get over here fast. It's seven o'clock, so we've got"—I looked at the clock—"four hours before the exterminators get here for the Fuzzles. That's not long."

"Not long to what?" Tomas asked, sounding a little more awake.

"To find a rogue Grim."

He sighed, as if I'd suggested this every day for the last week. "I'll be there in ten minutes."

Downstairs, Callie was already in the clinic answering the phone beside two dozen metal trash cans packed with Fuzzles—all the ones from Two Duck Lake, plus a few extras people had found that morning.

"Where's Aunt Emma?" I asked.

"She's in surgery. A Pawpig came in with a Lego stuck up his snout. Pawpigs," she scoffed, but she didn't sound like her heart was really into making fun of the Pawpig. She patted the nearest Fuzzle. It hummed.

"Hey—will she be in there long?"

"Do I look like I know how long it takes to de-Lego a Pawpig sinus cavity? She's got that meeting right after, anyway," Callie snapped, turning away.

Tomas arrived a few minutes later. His pockets bulged from the various inhalers, washes, sprays, bandages, and medicines he'd packed.

I lifted my eyebrows.

"What?" he said. "I wanted to be prepared. Grims can kill a man seventy-three different ways."

I lifted my eyebrows farther.

"We'll see who's laughing when you need my bandages," Tomas said solemnly. "So, where are we going?"

"The woods up behind Two Duck Lake. The Ducks saw the Grim, so I think that's where it is."

"We're walking all the way to Two Duck Lake? We don't have enough hours for that! And I should have brought blister pads . . ."

"Okay," I said in a low voice. "I don't want you to panic. But I think there might be only one way to make it to Two Duck Lake in time."

Tomas frowned. "Motorcycle? Jet Ski? Race car? I don't think I have the safety gear for any of those, but my brothers might."

I shook my head. "The only way we're going to make it to Two Duck Lake, Tomas, is on the back of a Unicorn. And there's only one Unicorn around here we can ask."

"No," said Regent Maximus. "No-no-no-no-no. You'll collapse my spine! I'll be a walking accordion! We'll get lost! I'll put my leg in a Groundfeatherdog hole! Oh, I'm too young to be maimed!"

Tomas looked relieved after I translated this response— he'd agreed to ask Regent Maximus, but clearly didn't like the idea of actually *riding* him. He sneezed into his elbow and said, "Well, that's settled, then!"

"No, it's not," I said. "Regent Maximus, I know you're scared. But this is important."

"Do you know what's important?" Regent Maximus asked me in a high-pitched whinny. He ran his lips back and forth over his stall bars. It made a *whub-whub-whub* sound and the Griffins in the other stalls laughed meanly. "Life is important! The pursuit of breathing is important! I don't want to die!"

"Neither do the Fuzzles!" I said. "You're a *show Unicorn*! You're supposed to be amazing! This is your chance to amaze! To be a hero! To prove to everyone you're more than . . . well . . ."

I trailed off, but Regent Maximus wasn't listening to me anyhow. He had stopped running his mouth over the bars and was instead tensing and untensing his lips. I could practically feel time ticking by. Maybe there was some other way to get to the lake. Maybe we could call a cab—I'd seen my parents do it twice in Atlanta, when they went to the airport. I didn't have my allowance here in Cloverton, but I knew where the pizza money was in the kitchen. I could borrow it, right? This was an emergency!

Except—no cab driver would take two kids to the middle of nowhere, even if they had money.

I thought about the Fuzzles trying to tell me what was chasing them. *Griimmmmmmmmm*. If only I'd figured it out sooner! If only I hadn't doubted my own ability to talk to them. If only I hadn't assumed they didn't have important things to say.

I took a deep breath.

"Look, Regent Maximus," I tried again. "I know you're scared. I'm a little scared too."

Tomas and Regent Maximus looked at me, like they were ready to be way *more* afraid after hearing this. I shook my head and my cheeks went warm. "It's just that

I did something dumb with Unicorns back at my school in Atlanta."

"Did a Unicorn *die*?" Regent Maximus gasped.

"No," I said. "It's just that I sort of got excited and didn't think about anybody else. I only thought about how cool it would be to ride a Unicorn and show off, and I ended up breaking a lot of things. I was so embarrassed and it was *terrible* and I never wanted to see another Unicorn again. Definitely not ride one."

I had Regent Maximus's full attention—his ears were pricked and, for once, I saw the resemblance between him and the Barreras' show Unicorns, because he was very handsome indeed. His intent expression made me feel both very important and very strange—no one had ever listened to me so closely. I kept going. "*So* I want you to know that I'm only asking you because I'm really afraid for the Fuzzles and this is the only way I can think of to get there. I don't have any other ideas. And I'm pretty scared that I might be wrong about asking you."

Tomas patted my shoulder and hiccuped a blue bubble out of my left nostril.

Regent Maximus quivered.

"I heard there are Bog Wallows at Two Duck Lake," he whimpered. My shoulders slumped, but then he added, "So if we go, I'm not going through any water."

"Agreed!" I said.

"Wait." Tomas looked at me strangely. "Did he say yes? Are we really doing this?"

Regent Maximus and I both bit our lips.

Tomas said, "At least let me pick up my bicycle helmet from the house."

Riding Regent Maximus was nothing like riding Raindancer. For starters, it took us ten minutes just to convince him to get close enough to the trash bins behind the clinic so that we could use one to climb onto his back. It was also strange having Tomas behind me—I'd already ridden and fallen from a Unicorn before, so I knew I could survive, but Tomas didn't seem quite as sturdy as I was. He seemed equally concerned, because he clung to me tightly enough that his hiccup bubbles kept popping on my ponytail.

Also, Regent Maximus didn't seem to have the same five gaits as the Barreras' Unicorns. He moved between slinking and scampering and ducking and shaking, depending on what we passed. For example—a bunch of dog water bowls? He scampered past those. A little sunflower-shaped windmill in a lady's yard? He ducked. The worst was when we passed a yard with three little yappy dogs behind the fence. I noticed them pretty early on, but thought—well, hoped—that maybe they were the watching sort of dogs, rather than the barking sort.

Unfortunately, they were the barking sort.

All three of them ran up to the fence, yapping and shouting and carrying on in squeaky little barks.

"It's okay, Regent Maximus!" I shouted. "They're behind the fence!"

But Regent Maximus was beyond comforting. He leaped up into the air and screamed, "They're going to gnaw my ankles off!" When he came down, his foot caught the edge of a garden bed full of sunflowers.

Tomas gripped me tighter. "Oh, no! I'm allergic to sunflow—"

He didn't get to finish, because Regent Maximus leaped again, all twisted, and Tomas and I went flying through the air. I saw the three little dogs beneath us, staring, as we arced over them. We hit the grass and rolled and rolled and rolled until we stopped with a little *oof*.

"Tomas!" I yelled the moment I could sit up. "Are you okay?"

"Yep!" Tomas said mournfully. "Except I'm also allergic to Chihuahuas." All three of the little dogs capered around him, licking his face and wagging their tiny tails. Tomas sneezed, and they scattered for a second, but then went right back to the licking. On the other side of the fence, Regent Maximus paced frantically.

"Sorry!" the Unicorn said. "Sorry, sorry! I didn't know what they were! Are they dogs? Are they monsters? Are they eating you, Tomas? Are you mortally wounded? Am *I*?"

I sighed. "No, we're okay. They're just dogs, Regent Maximus." I stood up and rubbed the spot on my butt where I'd landed. "All right, let's try this again."

We led Regent Maximus over to the quiet country road. We'd been trying to keep our distance from the road, because the noise of cars seemed likely to scare him, and because him spooking into traffic would be a lot more dangerous than him spooking into a field. But we were far from the clinic's trash bins now, so we needed the ditch beside the road to climb back on to his back. Tomas showed Regent Maximus that there was no water, ooze, or Bog Wallows in the ditch, and then the Unicorn stood in it, quivering, as we climbed back on. I quickly directed him back into the field, away from the road.

But Regent Maximus was clearly still freaked out by us falling. Or by the journey itself. Or by breathing. He was beginning to mutter to himself. And he was still shaking. I could tell he was only two seconds away from spooking again.

"I can't go on," Regent Maximus said. "It's all over. I'll never make it home alive. What am I doing? What was I thinking? I knew children were dangerous! I knew the world was full of things! I gallop into danger! I gallop to my end! When the gore—"

"Here's an idea," I told Regent Maximus. "Stop for a second. What if you close your eyes? Try it now."

I couldn't tell from his back if he was listening to me, but he stopped moving, and then he stopped talking. He stood, ears flicking rapidly from left to right. But slowly his breathing calmed and he stopped shivering.

"That's better," Tomas said. "But we're running out of time. We can't go anywhere with his eyes closed."

"Actually . . ." I said. "Maybe we can. I have an idea. Regent Maximus, do you think you can trust me?"

The Unicorn made a humming sound like a Fuzzle in response. I couldn't tell if it meant *yes*, *no*, or *I am very afraid of life.*

"I'm going to steer you with the reins," I said. "I won't let you get into trouble. I'll see the dangerous things and turn you away from them, and you don't have to see them and be scared."

I expected Regent Maximus to protest, but he nodded his head vigorously. I guess he thought it was less danger-ous to gallop about with his eyes closed than to face the world. Oh, well! I turned to Tomas and discovered his eyes were closed as well.

"Seriously?" I said. "I'm the only one looking where we're going?"

I was.

It hit me all at once: I was riding a Unicorn, just like I'd always dreamed about. And just like my first Unicorn ride, I'd talked my way into the situation. But unlike the Unicorn Incident, *this* Unicorn was listening to me, and I was listening to him.

Even though we still had a long way to go, I couldn't stop the grin from slowly spreading across my face.

And then I guided us all to Two Duck Lake.

CHAPTER
— 12 —

Things Get Grimmer

Two Duck Lake was surrounded by forest, so we had to leave Regent Maximus behind—he said he was afraid of the underbrush ("As if regular-sized trees weren't scary enough!") and I didn't think we needed to chance it, after our fall. Tomas suggested tying him to a stop sign, but I didn't want him to get eaten by a Grim if there was one here. So we snuck him into one of the crusty out-of-order public restrooms near the picnic tables. He stood obediently next to the sinks with his eyes still tightly closed, muttering to himself. His voice echoed off the tile.

"We'll be back soon," I promised him.

If we're not eaten by a Grim, I thought.

Then I shoved that thought aside and headed into the trees with Tomas.

Here was the thing about woods and me—I really loved animals and nature and all, but, deep down inside, I was from a city. We didn't have big stretches of trees and leaves and plants and little trickling rivers in Atlanta. We had parks, of course, but you couldn't really get lost in them because there were paths and signs everywhere.

So I kind of knew that being in the woods, where a Grim was lurking, with a boy who kept stopping to re-apply eyedrops—would be kind of scary.

And it was *really* scary, especially once we couldn't hear the sounds from the campground anymore. All sense of space and time vanished as we searched for clues.

"What time is it?" I whispered to Tomas, because it was so strangely quiet out here in the middle of nowhere that it seemed wrong to speak too loudly.

He studied his watch. "Ten o'clock." Then he sneezed for the fifty-third time.

It had taken a long time to coax Regent Maximus to the woods. Less time than walking, by a lot, but not as fast as I had hoped. And we'd spent way longer wandering in the woods.

We only had an hour left.

This was bad. I hadn't even seen a single black tuft of hair, much less an entire black dog.

"Have we been this way before?" I asked.

Something in the woods crunched in response.

Tomas and I looked at each other, then into the woods.

It was bright in here, being the morning and all, but it was still hard to see very far since there were so many leaves.

Tomas sneezed again, then clapped his hands over his nose at the sound of it. His eyes widened. "What if—what if I'm sneezing because it's close?"

"Tomas, you've been sneezing for a half hour—" I stopped. I looked at him, and my jaw dropped. The *Guide* said that Grims were "stealthy, slinky" animals. Half Ninja Dog, after all.

It was very possible that for the last half hour, the Grim had been following us. I took a deep breath.

"Hello?" I called out into the trees. "Any Grims out there?"

Nothing answered me.

But we did hear a light little crunch sound. Much too light to be a Grim.

I sighed, disappointed. And also a little relieved, because I didn't want to be eaten.

"Don't worry, Tomas," I said. "It's probably just a squirrel. Come on."

"I can't," Tomas replied, sneezing again.

"Tomas, you can walk and sneeze at the same ti—"

"No, I *can't*!" he protested.

I turned around to look and clapped my hand over my mouth.

Tomas was flying.

Okay, he wasn't flying. He was floating, the way a balloon does when it's nearly out of helium but has just enough left that you can't throw it away. His toes skimmed the moss on the forest floor.

"Tomas!" I said. "Get . . . get down!"

"I'm trying!" he said and kicked his legs like he was running. All that did was send him tumbling forward, spinning head over heels in the air, things cascading from his pockets. He flailed his arms around like a windmill before snatching on to my ponytail to steady himself.

Breathlessly, he gasped, "Thanks, Pip."

"Don't mention it." I winced as he tugged my ponytail harder. "Why are you floating?"

"I *told* you! I have allergies!"

"What are you allergic to that makes you float?"

Tomas, still floating over my head, ducked to avoid a low tree branch. "I don't know. Sometimes it's hard to tell what's making me have a reaction."

I pointed at his pockets. "Don't you have something useful in there?"

"Oh, right! I hope they haven't fallen out." With his free hand, he rustled in his pocket and pulled out some allergy capsules, which he swallowed quickly.

"How long do those take?" I asked.

"Fifteen minutes?"

Fifteen minutes is a very long time when you have less than an hour. And we'd lost some time with the floating and catching too. I was afraid to ask Tomas what time it was now.

"We have to keep moving. Just try to stay out of the tree branches, and hold on to my hair. It's our only chance of finding the Grim so—"

Crunch.

The sound was light, just like the last noise, but now it was much, much closer. Tomas eyed me from the air above my head.

I leaned toward the sound, peering through the leaves.

I saw a patch of black fur!

Jerking backward, I curled my toes in my shoes.

I tried not to think of all of the scary facts about Grims in the *Guide*.

"Hello!" I said again, this time not in a question voice. "I know you're there, Grim. My name's Pip, and I just want to talk with you."

I could feel Tomas shaking in fear—he was wiggling my ponytail. I couldn't blame him, especially as I heard more crunching—the Grim was approaching us. Grims must be *really* stealthy, I thought, for a huge animal like that to sound so light on the forest floor. Now there was more black among the leaves as it got closer, closer—

"Hi," the Grim said, finally emerging from the trees.

My mouth dropped open. I couldn't believe it! This was a Grim, all right—a big, black, magical dog, just like the *Guide* described. But this Grim wasn't the "size of a full-grown man at the shoulder." It barely came up to *my* shoulder.

Because this Grim? It was just a baby!

Juvenile Grim

CHAPTER
— 13 —

No Biting or Poking

The Grim sniffled a little, then hung his head low. He had burrs in his fur, and he looked a little thin. Everything about him was gangly and puppy-like, especially his big eyes.

"Hi," I said back. I was too shocked, at first, to say anything else. Then I asked, "Is the rest of the pack nearby?"

Tomas's shaking increased.

The Grim laid his ears back against his head. "I'm alone."

I asked, "What are you doing out here all by yourself? You're too young to be a rogue Grim, aren't you?"

The Grim opened his mouth, but instead of answering, he flopped to the forest floor. He put his head on his paws and let out a long, terrible whimper. Tearily, he said, "It wasn't my fault!"

There was nothing much sadder looking than a lost baby Grim weeping into a forest floor.

"Oh, hey, don't cry—" I started to stoop, but the closer I got to the Grim, the higher Tomas's allergies made him float.

"Hang on," Tomas said, grabbing hold of a tree branch overhead. When he had a secure grip, he released my ponytail. "Okay, I'm good!"

I rubbed the spot where my hair had been pulled and kneeled by the Grim. "I'm sure it's not your fault. What happened?"

It took a moment for the Grim to calm down enough to tell the story. He rubbed his nose on his paw. "My pack was asleep, but I heard something in the woods. I went to look, and there was this cat—it was huge! And so . . . I chased it, because that's fun, you know? But then when I stopped and looked around, I was . . ."

"Lost?" I suggested.

The Grim started to whimper again. He was making those big, ratty *snuff-snoooooooffff* sounds you make after you've been crying for a while. I very carefully extended a hand—he was a wild animal, after all—and patted him on the head. When I did, he crumpled toward me, a mess of black fur and paws and weight.

"Is he mauling you?" Tomas shouted from overhead. "I brought some hydrogen peroxide for the wounds!"

"He's not mauling me!" I called up, even though the

baby Grim *was* sort of suffocating me. He didn't mean it though, so I wrapped my fingers in his fur and patted him until he stopped crying.

"Listen," I finally told the Grim. "I bet I know where your family is. Grim packs migrate to the same place every year. My aunt will definitely know where the closest Grim migration point is. We can take you right to them!"

The Grim lifted his head to look at me, and I saw his very impressive bright white teeth. They flashed as he spoke. "Why would you help me?"

"Well, for starters, because it's a nice thing to do," I said. Gently, so that it didn't sound like an accusation, I added, "But also, because you've been eating Fuzzles, right?"

The Grim nodded and licked his lips. "They're all I can catch. I tried to catch regular food, *bigger* food, but . . . I'm just not fast enough yet . . ." His eyes wobbled like he might cry again.

"Okay, okay!" I patted him again. "Well, it's just that since you've been eating them, they moved into our town and keep burning things down. So once we reunite you with your pack, the Fuzzles will be able to come back to the wild. Everyone will be happy!"

"Except the Fuzzles I already ate?" the Grim asked.

"Well, yes, but let's not think about that," I said, cringing. "Stick with me and you'll be safe."

That was the moment Tomas's allergy medicine kicked in. He crashed to the ground beside us, emptying the remaining contents of his pockets. He bent to pick up the various packages of gauze and lip balms and spare batteries.

"Leave it! We have to go!" I said. We hurried toward the edge of the woods, which no longer seemed so far away or mysterious now that we had the baby Grim following us. As we reached the sunlight, I told Tomas, "Show me your watch!"

It was 10:35. The Fuzzles only had twenty-five minutes.

Tomas's shoulders slumped. "We'll never make it back in time!"

"If we go straight back!" I said.

"You know that won't happen! Regent Maximus will see a puddle or something and stop and *we'll never make it*!"

I couldn't believe it. We'd come all the way out here, found the Grim, and now the Fuzzles were still getting exterminated?

"No!" I said. "No way! Come on."

We ran to the bathrooms, where Regent Maximus was still waiting with his eyes closed. He seemed to be listing things he wasn't afraid of:

"Clouds, except not the ones that are dark or fluffy. Honeycomb, when it's not in hard pieces. Clouds. Honeycomb. Butterflies. Wait! No, not butterflies. Clouds . . ."

"Regent Maximus!" I said, voice a little louder than I meant to. His eyes flew wide-open. He looked at me, then at Tomas, then his eyes went even wider—the Grim was standing just behind us.

"He's going to *eat*—"

"No!" I said again. "Regent Maximus, this is a baby Grim. And he is lost and scared. Unless we get him back to the clinic, all of those Fuzzles are going to die."

Regent Maximus didn't seem swayed. Actually, he didn't seem *anything*. I think he might have been literally frozen with fear.

"Is he going to hurt me?" the baby Grim asked meekly, looking at Regent Maximus's horn. He was quivering a little. "Mom and Dad told me not to go near animals with horns. They're only used for poking."

Regent Maximus blinked. He screwed his eyes up at the Grim. For a moment, I thought he was preparing to run, but then he said, quite plainly, "Oh, you don't need to be afraid of *me*. Do I need to be afraid of you? Are you going to bite my ankles?"

"I don't bite ankles!" the Grim said, sounding offended. He leaned forward and very, very tentatively sniffed Regent Maximus's tail, then jerked back, still unsure.

I don't think Regent Maximus had ever met anyone who was so obviously afraid of *him*. He looked almost proud, really, and tossed his mane a little. He allowed us to lead him outside to the water fountain to get on his back.

"All right, Regent Maximus. Close your eyes!" I said. The Unicorn squeezed them shut. "We'll have to go fast this time if we want to make it," I added.

"I'll try," Regent Maximus said, shaking a little. "You'll warn me if there's something scary?"

"Absolutely," I said.

"And if *I* see something scary, I'll growl at it!" the Grim offered, wagging his tail a little.

So off we went, me and Tomas on Regent Maximus, the Grim running alongside us.

Hey, I thought, *we might just be able to save the Fuzzles after all!*

CHAPTER 14

Mrs. Dreadbatch Is Terrible People

We tore into the clinic parking lot at 10:55—the Fuzzles had five minutes left, by Tomas's watch! The Grim was drooling and Regent Maximus was panting and shaking his head. I *thought* we were going to slide off his back and run inside, but just as Regent Maximus slowed to a walk, the door of the clinic flew open.

Aunt Emma was the first one out. Then Callie. Then Mr. Randall. Then Mrs. Dreadbatch, and Mr. Henshaw, and that guy who had the Lilac-Horned Pomeranian, and Goggy's owners, and a bunch of other adults I didn't know.

Then the exterminators. Or at least, I guessed they were the exterminators—they had bright silvery suits on, with a tank of what I presumed to be Fuzzle poison on their backs.

They all stared at me.

"What's going on?" Regent Maximus asked anxiously. I guessed he could tell I was tensing up.

"Pip Bartlett!" Aunt Emma said before I could answer Regent Maximus. "You're in so much trouble!"

Mr. Henshaw's eyes were wide. I thought he was angry too, but then he lifted a wondering hand to Regent Maximus's bridle as Tomas and I slid off Regent Maximus's back. "I never thought I'd see the day! How did you manage this?"

That was a different conversation for a different time.

"Aunt Emma," I said urgently. "I know you're mad at me, and that's okay, but what about the Grim?"

Aunt Emma said, "What are you talking about?"

Mrs. Dreadbatch cut in before I could explain. "I don't have time for this, Emma Bartlett! The exterminators are here. Deal with your renegade niece later! Time to end this Fuzzle infestation once and for all!"

With that, the adults started arguing. Mrs. Dreadbatch shouted about the Fuzzles. Mr. Henshaw asked about Regent Maximus. Mr. Randall told Mrs. Dreadbatch to quiet down. Callie shouted at me for sneaking out and getting her in trouble. The other adults voiced a million opinions on the Fuzzles and the pending extermination and the risks of riding an unsaddled Unicorn down the street. Aunt Emma was stuck in the middle of it all, looking overwhelmed.

"Hey! Wait! Listen!" I said, but no one heard me.

"You'll have to speak louder than that, Pip," Tomas said.

So I took a deep breath and shouted, "I HAVE AN IDEA!"

It was loud enough that the adults settled down and looked at me. All their eyebrows were up high on their foreheads. I took another deep breath.

"We don't have to exterminate the Fuzzles, because it turns out they're only here because of *the Grim*!" I said, pointing to the baby Grim. He was crouched down near Regent Maximus, ears flattened back. "The Grim lost his pack, so he was wandering around eating Fuzzles. They only came into Cloverton to avoid being dinner!"

"A 'Grim'? You mean that dog? What is that, some sort of Labrador?" Mrs. Dreadbatch said. "I don't see any tags. If he doesn't have tags, we'll need to call Animal Control." She shot Aunt Emma a nasty look.

But Aunt Emma didn't notice—because she'd seen the Grim just long enough to know it was no Labrador.

Her eyes lit up. She looked like she might cry.

"Is that . . . Pip! You were right!" She dashed toward me. She nearly shoved Mrs. Dreadbatch out of the way as she dropped to her knees by the Grim's nose.

"Don't think you can convince me not to call Animal Control on that dog, Emma Bartlett!" Mrs. Dreadbatch snapped. "You might think you're in charge of magical creatures in this town, hiding Fuzzles and training Griffins and who even knows what else, but you can't save a regular old dog!"

"Oh, I think I can!" Aunt Emma held a hand out toward the Grim. He sniffed it and wagged his tail a little. I guessed dogs—even magical ones—can smell good people. "This, Mrs. Dreadbatch, is not just a dog. It's an extremely rare juvenile Grim. They're a protected species. And I'm the only person in Cloverton licensed to handle them."

She said this last bit with slightly more smugness than was absolutely necessary, but I think we all forgave her.

"Well . . . well!" Mrs. Dreadbatch said, hitching her blazer up a bit. "S.M.A.C.K.E.D. will be speaking with your niece, since she clearly is *not* licensed to handle Grims and brought him here! And in the meantime, the exterminators and I will go handle the Fuzzles—"

"Uh, about that," one of the exterminators said. "Sorry, lady, but we're not allowed to do anything that endangers a protected magical species. If that Grim-dog-thing eats Fuzzles, we can't touch them."

"*What?*" Mrs. Dreadbatch's eyes went all wide and buggy. "But they're pests! They must be exterminated! Stop! Don't you take another step! Don't you get in that van! Don't you start that—"

The exterminators slammed the van door—they looked eager to get out of Cloverton. When they turned the engine on, rock music blasted so loud that it completely drowned out Mrs. Dreadbatch's yelling. The tires squealed as they left the parking lot. Mrs. Dreadbatch huffed down the road after them. No one helped her give chase.

Mr. Randall spoke first. He said, "So this little fella is the only reason we've got a Fuzzle infestation?"

I nodded. "Now that he's not roaming the woods anymore, the Fuzzles should be able to leave."

"Pip is right," Aunt Emma agreed. "Sometimes one little thing can throw nature out of whack—like a rogue Grim hunting outside his normal habitat. I bet we can take the Fuzzles into the woods to release them now, and it'll be safe."

The adults talked about this for a moment. Some of the neighbors weren't totally convinced, but they were willing to give it a shot. Mr. Randall offered to take all the Fuzzles himself, since by this point he was pretty used to driving fireballs around. Everyone who'd gathered waved good-bye to the Fuzzles as Mr. Randall's truck disappeared over the hill.

"I will miss the marshmallows," Callie admitted.

Everyone filtered away—the neighbors back to their houses, Mr. Henshaw to put Regent Maximus up, and

Tomas home to tell his mom about the Fuzzles—and, I hoped, to brag a little to his brothers about the adventure he'd just been on.

"Pip," Aunt Emma said as she held the clinic door open for me, Callie, and the Grim, "I should have listened to you. I can't believe it was a Grim!"

"He lost his pack," I said. "I told him we'd take him to the Grim migration spot."

Aunt Emma stooped to pat the Grim's head. "You *told* him?"

I nodded. Aunt Emma didn't say anything for a moment. Then she said, "All right, then. I guess we are going on a road trip!"

I could tell she still didn't believe me about the talking part, but that was okay. She was happy, and I was happy, and the Grim and even Callie looked happy. The most important part wasn't to be believed. The most important part was that after ages of trying, I finally, really had been helpful!

What's a little Unicorn stampede here and there, if I can also help save five hundred Fuzzles and a baby Grim?

CHAPTER 15

A Chapter Where Absolutely Nothing Catches Fire, No One Is in Danger, Tomas Has Taken His Allergy Medicine, and Callie Is Perfectly Happy

I think if I had written the *Guide to Magical Creatures*, I would have included little sections with personal stories in them. You know, like how Bubbles got rescued by Aunt Emma. How Regent Maximus became brave enough to gallop rather than shiver. How sometimes HobGrackles want to learn ballet. Things like that.

This sort of seems like a missed opportunity to me, because I think there's a lot more to everyone than just the facts of their species. I mean, think about how different the stampeding Unicorns were from Regent Maximus! If there were personal stories in the *Guide*, readers would see that there's more to everyone than their average height, weight, temperament, and gestation period.

If I ever get to meet Jeffrey Higgleston, I'll tell him my idea and see what he thinks.

Anyway, if I was putting personal stories in the *Guide*, I'd include the one about the baby Grim and the Fuzzles. I'd talk about how Fuzzles aren't just pests, and are smarter than they look, and that baby Grims—just like baby anything elses—get scared when they're lost. I'd talk about us rescuing him and all that, but my favorite part of the story is the end.

We got to take the Grim back to his family ourselves! The American Academy of Magical Beasts offered to send someone down to get him, especially seeing how busy the clinic was. And for a few hours, it seemed like that was going to be the way it ended. It was okay, but I was a little disappointed. I had really, really wanted to be the one to bring the Grim back to the colony. What if he got scared in the crate on the way back? Who would tell him it was okay?

"But I can't leave the clinic," Aunt Emma said. "What if someone needs me?"

In the end, it was Callie who saved the day. By accident.

"Remember that favor you promised me?" she asked. "I want to use it. To go here."

She punched her finger right on a flyer for *Star Lady: The Musical*, which happened to be playing in Little Rover, North Carolina. Which *happened* to be just a few hours away from the Grim colony.

"That's a coincidence," Callie told me. "Don't look at me like that, Pip."

So we all piled into the car—Tomas included—and spent a whole day driving up there. Callie picked the music (*Broadway's Greatest Hits of Fall 1997*), and Tomas picked the food (it turns out Grims love french fries, but they give Tomas hives), and Aunt Emma quizzed me on animal facts.

It was the best day ever.

Once we got to the mountains of North Carolina, Aunt Emma pulled out the directions to the colony. We left the car behind and hiked up into the forest. Aunt Emma had her camera at the ready to document the reunion for the Academy.

"The directions aren't very specific," she apologized as we circled the forest. The trees around us were close together, and there were rocks everywhere thrown between them. Boulders, really. But not a Grim in sight.

The baby Grim made a little whimpering noise, and I rubbed his ears comfortingly. "I'm sure they're here somewhere."

"Definitely," Aunt Emma said, not realizing I was talking to the Grim. "Still—"

"Pip," squeaked Tomas. "Hold me!"

I grabbed him as he floated into the air. Aunt Emma lifted her eyebrows. Callie glared.

"Didn't you take your allergy medicine?" I asked.

"Of course I did!"

"Is it wearing off?" Aunt Emma asked. "I can't imagine it'd wear off so suddenly. I mean, if there were more Grims around maybe I'd understand—"

"Mom!" the baby Grim yelped. "Dad!"

He started running toward the rocks, still shouting. "Aunt! Uncle! Other aunt! Other uncle! Brother! Brother! Brother! Brother! Brother! Brother . . ."

Grims have large families.

He kept shouting to all of them as the rocks suddenly came alive. Well, not literally. But the other Grims had been lying on and around them, and when they saw the baby Grim galumphing toward them, they leaped up and galloped to meet him. We hadn't even noticed them. They blended in perfectly!

(I wrote a note on my hand about the excellent rock camouflage, since I clearly needed to add it to the *Guide*.)

They were all shouting and barking back and forth so loudly that I couldn't make out individual words. But I *could* make out my little baby Grim snuggling up against his parents, with his siblings all rolling around him gladly.

"Touching," Callie said. She looked at her watch. "Now can we go see the show?"

Lowering her camera, Aunt Emma wiped a tear away from her eye. "Of course."

Tomas muttered down at me, "I think this was a pretty good show already."

I grinned. It certainly was.

JACKSON PEARCE and MAGGIE STIEFVATER first met online through their shared love of reading, writing, and adorable animal photos. They have since become good friends and, despite living in different states, talk daily (to plan mischief) and visit each other often (to execute mischief).

With the Pip Bartlett series, they decided to join forces to tell the sort of story they wanted to read: one with clever kids, plenty of magic, and as many animals as they could fit onto the page. Maggie's favorite magical creature in the Pip series is the Scottish Bog Wallow; Jackson's is the Flowerbeast. This is their first collaboration.